White Wind

Spuds McCain is convinced the White Wind brings disaster to all those who sense its message, although Hobie Lee is sceptical. But bad things do happen to the Starr-Diamond Ranch and Hobie is hoodwinked and ambushed into trouble when his charge, Ceci Starr, disappears on a trip to town, and he falls foul of a loud-mouthed bully of a silver miner.

The White Wind blows away the rest of his common sense as he determines to restore the reluctant Ceci to her father, and it takes a maelstrom of death and double-cross before the White Wind blows itself out and Hobie can find peace.

D1422771

By the same author

Ghost Ranch
Comes a Horseman
The Outlaw's Daughter
The Lonesome Death of Joe Savage
Climax

White Wind

C.J. Sommers

A Black Horse Western

ROBERT HALE · LONDON

© C.J. Sommers 2014
First published in Great Britain 2014

ISBN 978-0-7198-1226-2

Robert Hale Limited
Clerkenwell House
Clerkenwell Green
London EC1R 0HT

www.halebooks.com

Typeset by
Derek Doyle & Associates, Shaw Heath
Printed and bound in Great Britain by
CPI Antony Rowe, Chippenham and Eastbourne

ONE

The snow was melted across the Dakota plains except for patches clinging to the dark folds in the hills and beneath the heavy stands of trees. The rivers were running full, fresh with snowmelt, though ice still decorated their fringes, clear and brittle, soon to be vanished from the landscape by the spring thaw. It had been a long hard winter; the high, drifting snow had kept man and beast alike sheltered away in their dens.

Now the sun was rising in clear skies; there was not a threat of further storms along the northern horizon, and the howling winds of winter no longer tried to force the planks of their winter shelters apart with cold, clawing fingers.

That is, in late March it had become early spring across the northland. The hands of the Starr-Diamond Ranch no longer wore their bulky buffalo coats, riding winter-shaggy horses as they patrolled the wide land, trying to save what cattle they could from the blizzards by herding them to sheltered areas and forking hay from the tall stake-bed wagons. The cowboys were more lively, cheerful, believing that in some way they had managed to defeat winter once again, when in truth they had just managed to survive it.

The land was coming to life once more. New grass could be seen, bright and green along the Kenasaw Creek, and the cottonwoods were budding. Other creatures had begun to stir from their winter lethargy. Hobie Lee had seen a grizzly bear with her two roly-poly cubs earlier in the week, pawing for fish in the Kenasaw. Twice a large pack of timber wolves had been seen trying to get at the cattle herd, and once a bold tawny puma had made its way to the yard of the Starr-Diamond looking for whatever it came across in the way of edibles.

Winter had retreated, but spring had brought its own challenges.

Predators of the human type had returned as well, skulking around the fringes of the ranch looking for loose cattle or free horses. Randy Dalton and Barney Keyes had gotten into a brief fire fight with a couple of suspected rustlers up along Sandy Creek days before. Both sides retired without evident injuries.

All of which only meant that the normal state of things had returned, awakened from its winter nap.

It was cold, clear, when Hobie Lee, who had been

repairing snow-broken pole fences beyond the south barn, returned to the bunkhouse for his noon meal. Cooky had corn bread and ham ready for the few men who would be able to make it in for the meal. Most of the crew were out on the far reaches of the ranch, looking for lost cattle. The winter kill-off of the steers had not been as large as they feared. The winter, though bitter, had been relatively short.

Hobie shrugged out of his buffalo coat and sat at the plank table of the bunkhouse kitchen, nodding his thanks to the gruffly silent Cooky for the cup of coffee he was served. Across the table Spuds McCain was pontificating on his favorite topic to anyone who would listen.

Mostly his speechifying drew yawns from the older hands like Calvin Winslow and Pump Grissom who had taken this opportunity to shed their boots and warm their feet by the iron stove which sat in the center of the bunkhouse.

The few younger hands like Randy Dalton and Gene Brady hunkered nearer listening to the older, wiser man's sermons.

'What I still don't understand,' Dalton was saying, as Hobie settled on to the bench opposite, 'is what causes this White Wind? I mean, there's got to be a reason behind it.'

'There ain't no known cause behind it,' the bulky, balding Spuds McCain answered. The older man's eyes were as intent as a preacher warning of hellfire, 'none that mortal man can comprehend. It comes in bearing its curse in bushel baskets, drives men to error, and some to madness.'

'Of which you are a prime example,' the red-bearded Pump Grissom said, barely lifting his eyes toward Spuds and his small audience. Pump was combing corn-bread crumbs from his beard with his fingers.

'Oh, and now you want to mock!' an animated Spuds said. 'As if you haven't seen enough of the White Wind's devil work in your time on the range.'

Pump only grumbled a response and inched his chair closer to the stove. Gene Brady, a fresh-faced, affable kid just up from Kansas, said, 'Call me slow, but I still don't understand what this White Wind is exactly.'

'It blows in on the heels of winter,' Spuds told the kid, resuming his sermonizing tone. 'Not every winter, mind you, but now and then and it carries a seed that makes men crazy, careless and wild.'

'I ain't felt no wind,' Randy Dalton said, sipping at his coffee. Cooky slammed down a tin baking tray in the kitchen, only briefly interrupting Spuds McCain's lecture. Spuds looked toward the ceiling of the bunkhouse, sighed with pity and leaned forward toward Dalton, his hands open in an imploring gesture. A professor with a room full of dull students.

'You don't *feel* the White Wind,' Spuds explained patiently. 'Not in the sense a normal wind is felt, that is. But you begin to look around you and notice men are doing wrong things, maybe hurting themselves and others, maybe seeming to briefly lose their minds!

'Then one day the wind has blown itself out and everything returns to normal. All I'm telling you young men is to watch out for the White Wind, because I fear it's blowing in strong this year.'

'I hear something blowing pretty hard,' Cal Winslow said. He was tugging on his boots now.

Calvin Winslow was a narrow, agreeable man with a thin mustache and careful manner. He was both yard foreman and trail boss on the Starr-Diamond.

'Don't say you never seen the White Wind blow,' Spuds McCain said defensively.

Calvin Winslow paused for a moment, pulling on his sheepskin coat. 'All I suggest is that you don't scare all of our new-hires off the ranch,' Winslow answered. 'How're those rail fences coming, Hobie?' he asked, swiftly switching subjects.

'I'll get 'em done tomorrow if not today,' Hobie Lee replied.

'All right – do you need any help?'

'A little help is always welcome,' Hobie said.

'OK. Why don't you go along with Hobie, Gene? You must have nailed those loose shingles to the barn by now.'

'Yes, boss. They're all secured. I'll go along with Hobie.'

9

'Fine.' Cal Winslow looked around. 'Pump? You're taking Randy back out along the Sandy, mavericking, right? Then everyone has enough work to fill in his afternoon. Stay warm and dry, boys, and if the White Wind starts to bother you, come back in and hide under your bunks until it stops.'

Cal managed not to smile as he started toward the bunkhouse door. Spuds McCain fell into a silent funk. Cooky was rattling dishes around in the tub, and the men were rising one by one from the table.

'We'd better get to it,' Hobie Lee said to the genial Gene Brady. 'I'm sorry it's not a saddle job.' Hobie was referring to the strong reluctance of a lot of cowhands to doing any task which could not be done from horseback.

'I ain't that particular, Hobie,' Gene answered, swallowing the last bite of his corn bread. 'Besides, I'm a new-hire and glad to have the job.'

The fence which began adjacent to the pig pen and ran in an irregular line toward the stable was not really necessary, but the boss, Gabe Starr, was fond of its look. It did keep out any horses or cattle who might have wished to stray into the area, but these had never showed any interest in the hog wallow and slops that Hobie could remember.

On foot the two young men walked toward the barn where the fence poles, ten-feet long, were stacked. Their job on that day was to replace the broken rails along the X-shaped supports. It was easy work, to be honest, but it was enough of a job to help shake the winter lethargy from their bones and get the blood flowing as it should.

In a few hours they had all of the old rails down and ready to be reused as firewood, and new rails placed across their frames. 'I can't believe that took something out of me!' Gene Brady said. 'The winter fat will take a little time to work off.'

'You do look like you've put on a few pounds since last year,' Hobie agreed.

'Once I'm back working cattle every day, it'll melt off,' Gene promised. He fanned himself briefly with his hat, though he couldn't have been warm. The day was cool, a teasing wind drifting through the oak trees in the yard, rustling the branches.

Before Hobie could stop him, Gene had backed up and seated himself on one of the long split rails of the fence. The rail splintered and collapsed under him and Gene found himself sprawled against the cold earth.

'How did. . . ?' Gene sputtered.

'Must have been that extra winter fat,' Hobie said, stretching out a hand to help Gene to his feet.

'Rotten rail is what it was,' Gene said, rubbing his hip.

'Didn't I tell you to check for rot before you selected the rails from the stack?' Hobie asked.

'If those rails were kept in a shed . . .' Gene said, groping for an excuse. The one he came up with was far-fetched. 'You don't suppose that the White Wind caused it, do you, Hobie?'

Hobie Lee was removing the broken rail from the fence. He had thought the job completed. Now they would have to trudge back to the barn, carrying the broken sections, and tramp back with a new rail and wire it down. It wasn't really that much more work, but Hobie was a little irked. Those rails were never meant to be sat on, and Gene should have known that.

'I asked . . .' Gene said, standing close behind Hobie as he used his pliers to undo the baling wire which had held the rail in position.

'Yes, I heard you,' Hobie answered. 'If the White Wind caused it. No, I don't. It's just some superstition Spuds decided to embellish at the expense of the green hands. It's like the man who walks under a ladder and gets the painter's bucket on his head – he blames his luck on the ladder. Let's forget about the White Wind and get this job finished. The actual wind is getting a cold edge to it.'

And the wind was indeed picking up, the skies growing rapidly dark. They trudged toward the warmth of the bunkhouse, relatively pleased with themselves. The day's labor had not been difficult, but they had accomplished as much as anyone could have. They felt they had earned their wages on that day, and were looking forward to a warm meal and a lazy card game as evening settled around them.

Making their way across the fallow cornfield they were rocked out of their pleasant, idle thoughts by the unmistakable report of a Colt .44 revolver close at hand. Hobie flinched, dropped his hand toward his own holstered pistol as a man nearby screamed in horrible anguish. Without caution, Gene Brady rushed toward the sound of the shot, his own sidearm in his hand.

They found the man down, writhing with pain not fifty feet this side of the bunkhouse. In the near-darkness they could make out the contorted features of Randy Dalton, who lay crumpled on the ground, clutching his leg, which was bleeding badly, staining his pantleg and the earth around him.

Others were arriving now from inside the bunkhouse. Pump Grissom carried his rifle, Barney Keyes was bootless, waving his Colt revolver around wildly. Behind them strode the yard boss, Calvin Winslow, his handsome face grim. Looking at Randy Dalton, then at Hobie, he demanded, 'Who did it?'

'Near as we can tell,' Gene Brady said, 'he must have done it to himself. We didn't see no one else around when the shot was fired.'

Pump Grissom, his broad face lined with concern, crouched beside Randy Dalton. 'Is it true, son? Did you shoot yourself?' Dalton's head barely moved in a nod.

'I thought I'd practice my fast draw while I had a little time to do it,' Dalton's pained voice responded.

13

Tully Sharpe had squatted to feel Randy Dalton's leg. He looked up to Calvin Winslow. 'Shattered the shin bone,' he told the foreman.

Spuds McCain had joined the crowd of onlookers. 'It figures,' the bearded man said. They all assumed that he was referring to the inevitable dark influence of the White Wind.

'Just shut up, Spuds,' Calvin Winslow said in an uncharacteristic flash of temper. 'Get him into the bunkhouse, boys. We'll see what we can do for him.'

A cold blast of air whipped its way across them; the darkening sky was gathering its strength for another frigid night. Cooky had emerged with a lighted lantern, but the wind defeated the sheltered flame and the lamp flickered out.

'Inside,' Winslow ordered again, and the men who had been standing around moved to scoop up the agonized Randy Dalton. With Tully Sharpe holding his shoulders, Hobie Lee supporting the bulk of Dalton's weight at the waist and Gene Brady holding Dalton's ankles, they managed to make their stumbling way back toward the bunkhouse and deposit the badly injured Randy Dalton on his bunk.

Cooky wasn't shy about using a butcher knife to cut away Dalton's new jeans so that they could examine his wounded leg. As Tully Sharpe had opined, Dalton's shin bone was shattered, his calf bleeding freely.

'Savage what a .44 slug can do at that range,'

14

Pump Grissom said, wiping his hand across his bald head.

'What do we do now?' was Calvin Winslow's question. 'What do you think, Cooky? Can you patch him up?'

'I've treated my share of broken bones, boss, but this is different. The man's leg is shattered. A splint won't even do him much good. As for recovering . . .' he murmured.

Angry at the situation, Winslow asked the feverish cowboy, 'Just what were you up to, Dalton?'

'Told you. . . .' Dalton's voice was weak. His eyes were closed. Sweat beaded his forehead. 'Practicing a fast draw . . . the pistol kind of got away from me.'

'You ought to leave that kind of game to men who know what they're doing,' Winslow said sharply. The yard boss was not angry with Dalton, they all knew, but at the result of the kid's poor decision. Winslow rose from Dalton's bedside. 'See what you can do for him, Cooky. I've got to talk to Mr Starr. He won't be happy about this.'

The night was clear and cold. Not a man slept well. Randy Dalton was whimpering or yowling all night. No one could blame him, knowing how badly he was injured. Still, as the night wore on men began to lose their tempers and send up futile curses from their bunks. Despite Cooky's ministrations, Dalton was no better at dawn. His leg was bound in a roughly fashioned splint; his face was waxy.

15

'Help me,' he muttered once as the men roused themselves for breakfast and the day's work ahead.

'The only help for you is to take your guns away,' Pump Grissom said sourly.

They were halfway through a mountain of scrambled eggs and thick-sliced toast when Cal Winslow entered through the front door and appraised his crew. Tully Sharpe and Barney Keyes were the first to shove their tin plates away, and so Cal spoke to them at the side of the kitchen.

'If the word hasn't already leaked down here somehow, boys,' Calvin Winslow said, 'the boss wants fifty prime beef cut out of the herd. And he does mean prime. The sleekest and fattest of the winter survivors.

'Osborne is waking up from a long winter, too,' Cal continued so that every man could hear him. He was referring to the nearest town, Osborne, which worked closely with the Starr-Diamond, providing the ranch with all of the items the SD could not manufacture itself, from blankets to frying pans. In return the town was a prime market for SD beef.

'Their butchers are getting lazy, and with a few more weeks of warmer weather, those silver mines up above the Knob will be opening again. We're taking steak on the hoof over there tomorrow morning, and the boss says nothing but the best is going. It's the SD's reputation that it delivers only prime beef.'

'I don't know if there's fifty steers out there with

16

enough fat on them to be considered prime after the winter we've had,' Tully Sharpe said.

'There are,' Cal Winslow said with an edge to his voice, 'and you and Barney are going to start culling them this morning. The rest of the boys will be along to help with the gather and drift them toward the pens.'

Cal Winslow leveled his gaze at each man in turn, 'That's the way Mr Starr wants it, and you will get it done by evening and be ready to push the herd to Osborne tomorrow morning. It's time you started paying the boss back for your winter shelter and grub.'

Hobie glanced at Gene Brady. They had never heard Winslow talk like that before, but then the foreman had a point as did the boss, Mr Diamond: they had done nothing much over most of the long winter but eat the ranch's food and play cards. A man has to pay for his days of leisure sometime.

Around the table, men lingered or rose to find their boots. Hobie had thought that Winslow was through with his speech, but he had one more thing to say.

'You two,' he indicated Hobie Lee and Gene Brady, 'you won't be riding out with the crew this morning. Mr Starr wants to see you.'

'Us?' Hobie's first thought was that he was going to be let go, but that made no sense. At this time of year finding new hands was nearly impossible. It was not until the warmer weather set in that rambling cowboys, dragging the line looking for work, would start to drift this way.

'As soon as you get your pants on,' Cal Winslow said. 'I'm stepping outside for a smoke.'

Winslow turned on his heel, walking toward the front door of the bunkhouse, his hand fishing for the tobacco pouch in his shirt pocket. Hobie and Gene stood there for a moment, confused.

'Why us?' Gene Brady asked no one in particular.

'Probably 'cause you ain't no use otherwise,' Barney Keyes gibed, stamping his feet into his boots.

Hobie tried to be philosophical. 'There's only one way to find out,' he said, resting his hand on his friend's shoulder, 'and we'd better get started. Calvin Winslow isn't the kind to wait long.'

The yard boss was just toeing out the stub of his cigarette when Hobie and Gene Brady emerged from the bunkhouse into the crisp air of morning. Cal Winslow simply nodded, tugged down his hat and started out toward the two-story white house with its green trim which was the home of Gabe Starr, the owner of the Starr-Diamond.

Hobie had never so much as seen the man, although through bunkhouse gossip, exchanged over the long course of a blanketing winter, he knew something about him. As a young man Starr had drifted up out of Amarillo, Texas, farther and farther into the north country with his friend and partner,

Lucas Diamond, looking for free range. When they came upon the open grassland spread out across what was now the SD ranch, with water flowing freely, they had decided to make their stand.

Years of driving cattle up all the way from Texas or Kansas, suffering through the freezing winters, sheltering in crude huts and worse had taken the urge for ranching from Lucas Diamond and he had chosen to sell out to Starr and move someplace where the sun shone more warmly and the only beef he saw was on his platter.

But Gabe Starr was put together differently. He had started this ranch and he meant to finish with it, come what may. No one would ever know what the old man endured in his earlier years, but he now was financially secure and comfortable as far as anyone could tell. When the town of Osborne had first begun to be built to service the silver mines being dug up along the area they all knew as the Knob, a long low stretch of hills to the north, Starr had immediately recognized the opportunity. Their cattle, or a good share of them, could be driven a mere fifty miles and sold at a handy profit in Osborne Town. The townspeople were equally pleased with the arrangement – the men making the long cattle drives in from Platte and even Colorado had to consider the distance and time involved when setting their prices. These long-drivers had to consider the food required, replacement horses, Indian raids, their trail losses and time spent away from the home ranches in their bargaining. Starr was much nearer and more willing to meet the town's requirements.

And he made a healthy profit from his nearly exclusive arrangement with Osborne, as did the traders there who sold their beeves to the mining companies at a not inconsiderable mark-up. The mining men had no complaint coming. They needed the beef to keep their men working, and silver was getting more profitable with each passing year as methods of extracting the mineral from the ore improved and the government kept on coining silver money. Bunkhouse chatter had it that the Denver mint alone was stamping ten million silver dollars a year. Hobie knew nothing about that, but it was certain that a not inconsequential portion of the silver used was being mined along the Knob.

Calvin Winslow indicated a muddy puddle beside the house without speaking and Hobie and Gene Brady side stepped to avoid it. It wouldn't do to go tracking mud into the boss's house on their first visit. Despite Winslow's warning Hobie wasn't quick enough to avoid the mud entirely and he spent a few minutes cleaning his boots on the scraper fixed on the house's porch. Winslow had removed his hat, and so Gene and Hobie followed suit. In front of the house, a dozen or so budding elms shivered in the wind. The skies remained clear, but the air felt heavy.

The door was suddenly swung open by a very small

man named Cabo. Nearly a midget, the dark man had been houseboy on the Starr-Diamond for nearly ten years. With a slight bow, Cabo allowed the three ranch hands to enter.

TWO

The interior of the house was of a familiar type –
stone fireplace and thrown Indian rugs on the hardwood floor. The furniture was of heavy, dark Spanish
wood with black cushions. Beside the mantel was a
gun rack holding older weapons than a man usually
saw, probably remembrances of time past: a
Sharps.56, a Spencer with a splintered stock, an army
Springfield rifle, bayonet fixed. A curved staircase
led to the upper story where the bedrooms would be.
From a kitchen Hobie could not see, the tempting
scent of what he took to be beef stew drifted.

Gabe Starr himself stood at the side of the stone
fireplace, his intent, expressionless blue eyes watching them from beneath extravagantly bushy white
eyebrows. Starr was not thin but lanky, wiry as they
say. His hands seemed too large for his body, and
they were tanned, gnarled from years of hard work,
strong appearing. He gave the impression of a man

approaching old age with a challenge.

A door opened upstairs and Hobie glanced that way but saw no one. The door closed again and Starr said, 'Good morning, boys; have a seat. Did Calvin tell you what I need you for?'

'I thought I'd leave that to you, sir,' Cal Winslow said. 'Before you start, though, I have to report that a couple of the men thought they spotted Hal Bassett up along the north wood line.'

'And they didn't hang him?' Starr asked coldly.

'No, sir, they weren't sure it was him. He never came that close.'

'The man is trying my patience. If he came back, Calvin. . . .' Starr fell silent. His eyes were blazing now; it was a cold fire, and Hobie was glad the ranch owner's dark emotions weren't directed at him. Whoever Hal Bassett was, it seemed he would be wise to keep clear of the SD. Hobie sat uneasily beside Gene Brady on one of the two black leather sofas. They exchanged an uneasy glance as Starr came closer to look them over.

'So these are the ones, are they?' Starr asked Calvin, who nodded.

'You said you wanted two of the newer men.'

'So I did,' Starr replied with a small sigh. 'Either of you two know Hal Bassett? Ever met him?'

'No, sir,' Hobie and Gene said at the same time.

'Didn't see how you could, but you never know,' Starr said, looking again at Cal Winslow. 'I know you're wondering why you're here, boys. It's like this – as you know we're driving fifty prime beef over to Osborne town in the morning. You two are going along, but not as drovers. We've plenty of experienced men to handle the drive.'

'Then what—?' Gene began, but automatically silenced himself. Starr would tell them in his own way, in his own time.

Starr glanced at a chair, seemed to decide this was not the time for sitting and told them, 'Men, my daughter, Ceci, has been stuck in the house over the long winter. She heard about the trail drive and begged me to let her go along to Osborne to buy some new dresses and other things a woman needs. Well,' Starr said, scratching his head, 'it seems like a reasonable request, but I don't like her riding loose with the herd. I thought about asking her to use the buckboard, and when Calvin told me we have a man with a self-inflicted gunshot who needs to see a doctor, it kind of hardened my resolve.

'You two boys will handle the wagon – at least, one of you will; Calvin will tell you later what's expected. You will take Ceci and the wounded man – what's his name, Calvin?'

'Randy Dalton,' Calvin Winslow said.

'Oh, yes. I remember him. Not a bad hand as I recall. Helped Barney Keyes chase off a couple of rustlers the other day, didn't he?'

'That's the man,' Winslow confirmed.

24

'Sorry he got himself shot. We'll get him to Osborne to see a doctor.' He returned his attention to Hobie and Gene Brady. 'That's the job, men: you will get this man to Osborne to have his wound treated, and you will see that my daughter reaches Osborne safely. And,' he said forcefully, 'that she returns safely.

'I wanted two younger men for the job because first of all, they were unlikely to have ever met Hal Bassett and have had any dealings with him, and second because some of the older hands, some of them very good men on the trail, are likely to throw all caution to the winds and forget what they're about once they get within sight of a saloon. I don't begrudge them their drinks, understand, they've had a long winter as well. I understand that, and I tolerate it. But my daughter, Ceci, must be escorted around Osborne – it can be a dangerous town. And now with the word that Hal Bassett might have come back, it's especially important.

'Bassett is a very bad man, boys, and he believes that Ceci may be his for the taking. You are to make sure that nothing like that happens. No roughneck in Osborne is to approach her and, if Bassett even tries, you are expected to kill him dead.'

Hobie only nodded although his mouth was dry. Had he just been ordered to commit murder?

'That's all for now, boys,' Starr said, wearing a grim little smile. 'Don't let me down. Calvin? Did you have

25

the chance to tell these boys what I will do to them if they let me down?'

Calvin Winslow replied, 'I find that it's kind of hard on my stomach to even repeat those details,' and Hobie noticed that there was no hint of humor in the foreman's eyes.

'Well, leave out the details, then,' Starr said, 'just make sure that they understand.'

'I'll see that they do,' Winslow promised.

Hobie and Gene Brady left first while Winslow lingered a while longer with Gabe Starr, discussing the cattle drive.

'The boys were all convinced we were finding an easy way out of work,' Gene said. 'Me, I'm not so sure.'

'Neither am I,' Hobie answered. 'But probably nothing will happen. We'll have the crew along with us, after all. The old man just wanted to make us understand how important his daughter's safety is to him.'

'I guess you're right,' Gene agreed. 'I sure got the idea.'

'So did I,' Hobie said. 'The first thing—' His words halted as Gene stopped, standing stock-still in his path. 'What is it?' he asked roughly. 'I nearly walked into you.'

'Hobie, look up at that window, would you?'

Hobie turned and raised his eyes. In an upstairs window they could see a woman. Her face was like

26

that of a tiny porcelain doll, but her body was that of a full-grown woman. Her hair was brushed, falling free across shoulders and breast. Sparkling blue eyes briefly swept over them and a tiny smile lifted the corners of her mouth. Then the window curtains fell shut. They had had their first introduction to Cecilia Starr. Gene Brady said what was on Hobie's mind:

'I'm getting a nervous feeling about this job, Hobie.'

One thing was plain: why Gabe Starr was so protective of his daughter. And why Hal Bassett, whoever he was, was so eager to reunite with Ceci.

Hobie and Gene Brady were not the only men who chose to sleep in the barn that night. Randy Dalton, his leg now horribly inflamed, rolled and screamed and moaned in his bunk.

'Well, come morning he'll be on his way to the doctor in Osborne,' Hobie told the men gathered around him on makeshift beds of strewn straw.

'We should just put him out of his misery,' Barney Keyes grumbled. 'I had a hard enough day. I was looking forward to sleeping on my own bunk.'

Pump Grissom was gathering hay for his own bed. 'Is that what you want us to do for you if you happen to break a leg?' Pump asked, spreading his blankets.

'If I'm dumb enough to shoot myself in the leg, yeah,' Keyes said. 'I'd deserve it.'

'What's this we hear about Hal Bassett being back?' Gene Brady asked. He was propped up on one elbow, his young face drawn with some concern.

'Who says Bassett is back?' Tully Sharpe wanted to know. The old hand was frowning deeply.

'Calvin Winslow for one,' Gene answered.

'It's true,' Heck Booth told them. 'Me and Trager spotted him just yesterday a little beyond the Kenasaw.'

'There's a man who deserves killing,' Pump Grissom said. 'Are you sure it was him?'

'Sure as I could be without him coming up and introducing himself,' Heck Booth said.

'What is it everyone has against Hal Bassett?' Gene wanted to know.

'What?' Trager repeated with a choking laugh. 'The man's a swaggering bully.'

'Who cheats at bunkhouse poker,' Tully Sharpe chipped in.

'And will lie to his best friend – assuming he had one.'

'He's a well-qualified snake.'

'And Cecilia Starr fell for him?' Hobie Lee asked.

'She's a female,' Pump Grissom answered. 'What would she know, except that he is a handsome dog, and when he puts his manners on he can be a charmer. He'll charm you out of your socks.'

'Then laugh in your face,' Sharpe said.

'No, sir, the man is just no good. He's a thief, a liar, a braggart, without a warm bone in his body. Charmed his way in here, but you can only fool old

Gabe Starr for so long. When Gabe had had enough, Bassett was run off, and there wasn't a man here who wasn't happy about it.'

'Why would he come back here,' Hobie asked, spreading his hands, 'where he's not wanted?'

'You already know, but I'll tell you again: Ceci Starr, of course.'

'He cares that much about her?'

'Her and the SD Ranch. Gabe Starr can't live forever.'

'He would string her along, marry her just to get the ranch?' Hobie asked with wonder. He supposed he was still an innocent, but such a plan struck him as criminal.

'Sure, it would be an easy way to riches, and Bassett always takes the easiest way,' Pump said.

'It won't turn out to be so easy if Gabe Starr runs across him,' Gene Brady said. 'And Cal Winslow told him that Bassett was around the area.'

'Of course he would be back,' Spuds McCain, who had been standing near the barn door, smoking his pipe, said. 'It's the time of the White Wind, and it has blown trouble our way once again.'

'Oh, shut up, Spuds!' Pump Grissom said, rolling over and pulling his blanket up over his head.

'Go ahead and scoff, boys,' Spuds said, 'but the White Wind is blowing, and it's going to blow hard this year.'

*

29

Hobie and Gene Brady were the last ones up in the morning. The other men were out gathering the prime cattle and herding them in one of the pens where Calvin Winslow would make the final selection of those to be driven to Osborne. When Gabe Starr said that he wanted only the finest of the winter herd delivered, he meant it.

After a hasty breakfast Hobie Lee and Gene selected two horses to pull the wagon that would be used to transport the injured Randy Dalton and Cecilia Starr to town. Calvin Winslow stopped by just as they were finishing harnessing the animals. The foreman stopped his glossy black horse and leaned low to tell the two men with some intensity, 'This trip must be made safely. I think the boss made that clear. I recommend that one of you – Hobie – act as an out-rider to keep a watch for any trouble and Gene, you handle the team.

'Stay well away from the herd, and if any cattle try to break out of it, you just let them go, Hobie. That is none of your job. Your only duty is to transport Dalton . . . and to make sure no harm comes to Miss Cecilia either along the trail or in Osborne once it is reached.

'You both do understand that, don't you?' Winslow asked sternly. 'No gambling, no drinking, no galli-vanting for you two in town. You are not to leave Miss Starr's side, no matter what she says. She might spark and fume a little, say she's old enough to take care of herself, she might even try to charm you into letting her have her way, but you stay close to her no matter what.'

'We understand you,' Gene said.

'Good, now get back to the bunkhouse, throw a mattress into the wagon bed and put Randy Dalton in back. Then come by the big house; Miss Starr will be waiting. The herd should be started by then. Stay within hailing distance of it, but out of the trail dust. Is that all clear?'

'Perfectly clear,' Hobie answered, buckling the last harness strap on his side of the team. 'I'll just get my horse and then we're ready to go.'

'Fine. Boys, don't let me down. I'd hate to see all of our careers on the SD end because of a mistake on your part.'

Winslow started his horse back to where the herd was gathered. Hobie re-entered the barn and led out his paint pony. Gene had stepped up on to the wagon's bench seat. They exchanged a brief look and started back toward the bunkhouse to collect the injured Randy Dalton.

Hobie brought an unused mattress from the bunkhouse and placed it on the wagon bed. Then with Cooky's help they carried the groaning Randy Dalton to the wagon. Dalton's face was bloodless-appearing, sheened with perspiration. As Hobie was spreading a blanket over the wounded man Dalton's eyes flickered open.

'Where are you taking me?'

'To town to see the doctor.'

'About time!' Dalton said with a sickly smile. 'Hobie, I thought maybe you were taking me to the cemetery.'

'Not yet,' Hobie said as cheerfully as he could.

'Halting his horse beside Gene Brady, who sat on the bench seat holding the reins to his team, Hobie said, 'The big house next – we've got to pick up Miss Cecilia.'

'I know it,' Gene said dourly.

'What have you got to look unhappy about?' Hobie asked. 'You're taking a ride with a beautiful girl on a sunny day.'

'I know, Hobie. Still, I think I'd be happier pushing the steers.'

'Well, you're not going to. Any of those men would be happy to trade places with you.'

'It's just that I've got this kind of uneasy feeling, Hobie.'

'Don't start blaming the White Wind.'

'I'm not blaming anything,' Gene replied, 'but I just don't like this job.'

Hobie didn't like it much himself, but he said nothing further to Gene about it. They started the wagon forward and within a few minutes drew up at the front of the Starr house. Ceci's traveling bag was on the porch, but there was no sign of the girl. She must have been waiting inside for them. The houseboy, Cabo, appeared in the front doorway and called that Miss Ceci would be right out. Starr himself looked out the door but he said nothing to them, nor did he so much as wave. The man was concerned; that much was obvious.

Hobie's paint pony pawed impatiently at the earth, ready to be moving on. In a minute Ceci, accompanied by her father, appeared on the porch. She was wearing a tan-colored dress, a white western hat and a striped shawl over her shoulders. Starr had picked up the travel bag and was walking toward them, Ceci on his arm.

Assisting Cecilia as she clambered up on to the wagon's bench, Starr managed to flicker a warning glance at Gene Brady and Hobie. They had *better* be up to the job. Gene started the team and Ceci waved and gave her father a cheerful goodbye. Then she settled back as Gene guided the team through the oak trees in the yard and out on to open land where they could see the herd of steers making its slow way across the wide land toward the town of Osborne. The wagon hit a rut and Randy Dalton groaned. Cecilia glanced back, her look one of surprise at finding Dalton there, although she must have been told that they were transporting Randy to the doctor in Osborne.

They were near enough to the recalcitrant herd that Hobie could make out Calvin Winslow on his leggy red roan riding point, Tully Sharpe and Trager riding flank on this side and Booth and Pump Grissom riding drag. It appeared to be hard work getting the animals lined out after their winter of freedom. More than one steer balked and tried to escape from the herd only to be driven back into it by the cowhands on their quick-cutting horses.

Gene thought he would prefer being over there, working cattle unused to the trail, but did he? Hobie returned his attention to the wagon. Ceci seemed to be animated. She was smiling, chatting as the breeze drifted her dark hair. Gene Brady had the tight expression of a mummy. What was the matter with the kid? Probably he was just tongue-tied at Ceci's proximity. Hobie had to admit that he, himself, might feel as tense and uncertain in such circumstances.

Hobie Lee let his eyes shift to the distances. There were pine trees along the verge of the hills to the north, nothing but amber grassland patched with snow to the south. He saw no one, expected to see no one. It would take a bold band of rustlers indeed, to hit the herd with ten armed men riding watch over it. As they had discussed, it was too early in the year, right on the heels of the winter storms, for roaming gangs to be wandering the northland looking for easy pickings.

But a lone man? It was apparently not too early in the year for Hal Bassett to have made his return. Was Bassett unaccompanied, Hobie wondered? No one had mentioned any other riders having been seen with him, but you never knew, he supposed. At any rate there was no one around in the middle of the cool, clear afternoon as they made their way westward. There was only the slow, steady squeak of a wheel hub which should have been greased before they left – neither man had thought of that – and the lowing of the unhappy steers accompanied by the occasional shout of a cowboy.

Therefore it was quite inexplicable to Hobie that he himself felt as if he were riding into trouble. What could happen? At the first sign of any arriving strangers, the cowboys would abandon the herd if need be and rush to protect Gabe Starr's daughter. Still there was a lingering uneasiness in the air. Hobie shook his head; he was getting a superstitious as Spuds McCain.

The unhappy, weary steers were pushed across a shallow creek known as the Corken and pushed onward. At the hour before sunset they could see the small, squat forms of the dark buildings in Osborne town; they had arrived ahead of schedule. There should be time to get the cattle safely penned up before nightfall. The hands would be relieved, ready to do a little celebrating with their task ended.

Hobie's job was only beginning, he knew.

The drovers could pen up their charges, knowing that they were secure for the night, in the hands of other men. Hobie could not pen in his charge. Cecilia Starr was going to do what she wanted to do, go where she wanted to go. He and Gene Brady could only hope to follow and protect her wherever that was.

Osborne did not have the reputation of being a tough town, but when the men got to drinking and a beauty like Cecilia Starr strolled by, she would not go unnoticed. The townsmen, most of them, had women and children at home. Not so the miners who were now arriving in town. These were a rough crude bunch as Hobie knew from their arrival last year. They would have to stop over in Osborne to stock up on supplies. Undoubtedly a few of them would take advantage of this last opportunity to throw themselves a party before the weeks, months of hard labor at the Knob's silver mines began.

And Hal Bassett? Of him there had been no sign, but if he had been lurking around the SD, he could not have failed to notice the trail herd being gathered, its departure and the accompanying wagon carrying Cecilia Starr. It was now that Hobie altered his opinion to match that of Gene Brady – they would have been better off driving cattle than babysitting Cecilia Starr. Entering the town limits as sunset colored the western skies with flaming crimson and orange, Gene halted his wagon team and motioned Hobie over.

'Well, what do you want to do? I've got to get Randy to the doctor's office – I don't think he can take much more.'

'I have to find a place to wash up and change my clothes,' Ceci said. There was nothing whiny about her words, but her method of speaking was that of one who expects to have her every wish obeyed. Maybe she had been raised that way, being the only child of a powerful man.

'Look up ahead,' Hobie said, pointing. 'That two-storey building on the corner is the Osborne Hotel if I remember correctly. Drop Miss Cecilia off there. I'll see to it that she has a room, dinner, whatever else she wants. You take Randy directly to the doctor's. There will be someone around who can help you carry him in.'

'I really don't need an escort to check into a hotel,' Ceci complained. 'I'm a big girl.'

'I realize that, Miss Cecilia, but we've been told not to leave you on your own in town.'

'Oh, ho!' she said. There was a crooked little smile of amusement on her lips. 'So that's how it's going to be, is it?'

'I'm afraid so. That's the way things have to be if we want to hold on to our jobs.'

'All right. Give me a hand down, then,' Ceci said. 'If you think it's safe for me to walk two blocks alone in this demons' hole.'

Tying his horse loosely to a nearby hitch rail, Hobie offered his hand to the lady and watched as she swung down from the wagon, her skirts billowing. Then Hobie retrieved Ceci's bag from the bed of the wagon. He paused to say 'Goodbye, good luck' to Randy Dalton, but the injured cowhand didn't so much as twitch a finger.

'Better get Randy over to the doctor's right now,' Hobie said.

'That was my intention,' Gene said drily. He was still peeved – whether at Ceci, the job, or at Hobie's unnecessary advice could not be determined.

The wagon rolled away heavily and Hobie turned toward the plankwalk . . . to find Miss Cecilia Starr missing.

THREE

Hobie was never much of a man for cussing – he figured bad language was a waste of breath and an embarrassment for the speaker, but just then he squeezed a few choice words out between his lips as he looked down the street to find it bare of pretty little women. Where had she gone? Probably to the hotel, though it didn't seem she'd had enough time to vanish like that on a public street.

Muttering to himself, Hobie carried the heavy travel bag to his pony and mounted awkwardly – what did the girl have packed in the bag? Walking the paint along the street toward the hotel, he paused to glance into each alley, though he couldn't under-stand why Ceci should have ducked away into one of them. Unless she was already trying to ditch her escort and meet up with someone – like Hal Bassett. Hobie's throat constricted a little. If he had lost Ceci, Calvin Winslow would have his hide and there was no telling what Gabe Starr would do besides booting Hobie off the SD. He brightened a little as he reflected that the girl would not have abandoned her travel bag – at least he didn't think so.

Swinging down in front of the hotel, which was of two stories, white-painted and just now blossoming with lantern light beyond the front-facing glass windows, Hobie went into the chandelier-lit lobby. There she was. It was relief mingled with anger finding her there. Ceci was seated on a red-plush settee against the wall, hands folded together demurely on her skirt.

'There you finally are,' Ceci said, rising.

'You shouldn't have walked off like that,' Hobie said, tension throttling his words.

'Are you afraid to be alone?' she asked in a mocking tone. 'Look, whatever your name is, I told you that I was a big girl and could manage to walk two blocks by myself.'

'Hobie.'

'What?' Ceci asked, puzzled.

'My name is Hobie, Hobie Lee,' he said stiffly.

'Fine,' she replied breezily, rising to her feet. 'You already know mine. Let's find a room for me, shall we, *Hobie*?'

He didn't care for the way she emphasized his name, but this was no time for sensibilities. The thing to do was get her settled, fed and tucked in for the night. The hotel lobby was crowded with townsfolk in their finery, a cowboy or two crossing the lobby and along one wall a group of newly arrived miners in twill trousers or shabby overalls and leather caps. These early arrivals would be waiting for their boss, hoping to get the prime jobs by being first on the scene. The snow had mostly cleared, but there was no way of telling when the Knob mines would be ready to open. Maybe the mine owners had been waiting, among other things, for the arrival of the SD beeves.

The prim little man with the red bow tie behind the counter was not busy, but trying hard to look as if he were. Hobie started to speak, but Ceci took over immediately.

'I require your finest suite and a bath to be sent up to it.'

'Suite?' The desk clerk blinked as if he had never heard the word before. Maybe he hadn't in this edge-of-the-civilized-world hotel where the usual guests were beat-down trail drivers and local singles. The influx of miners would bring the hotel an increase in guests at least for a few days more, but the hotel probably had a tough time making a go of it in the normal course of events.

Hobie took a hand in matters. 'This is Miss Cecilia Starr,' he told the clerk, emphasizing the last name slightly, 'and she wants your finest accommodation.'

'Miss Starr,' the clerk said, stuttering just a little. 'Of course, of course.'

41

He turned the register and Cecilia signed it with a rather girlish flourish. 'Do not forget my bath,' she reminded the man, 'and that should be started immediately.'

'We have water heating at all times. I'll have the boys carry the tub up right away.'

Ceci didn't bother to thank the man; she turned away from the counter as soon as she was given the key to an upstairs room and walked toward the staircase, Hobie following like a faithful servant. There was not a man in the lobby who did not give her a glance as she passed. A few were not ashamed to stand and stare. Hobie wished that Gene Brady would return so that he could find a way to shift the job into Gene's hand, but his business at the doctor's office might take quite a while.

The hotel room was pleasant, but in no way could be considered a suite. Hobie doubted that the hotel had such a thing: the establishment was frontier-designed for the frontier trade. The walls were cream, the carpet a dark blue. An arched window opened on the alley side, the bed was brass with a multi-colored coverlet and there was a mahogany washstand with basin and ewer and an oval mirror hanging above it.

Hobie had never spent the night in such a room and doubted that he ever would. But then he didn't have Ceci Starr's money.

'Where do you want your bag?' he asked.

'Are you still here?' Ceci asked, turning away from the window where she had parted the sheer curtains to look out at the night.

'Where do you want the bag?' Hobie repeated stiffly. He was no servant despite their current situation and resented being treated like one.

'Anywhere,' was her only answer as she sat on the bed. Two men with a good-sized copper tub were at the hallway door and they entered, placing the tub down with a clatter.

'Water's on the way,' the older of these two said.

The men lingered as if waiting for a tip, but Ceci made no move toward her purse. After futilely looking toward Hobie, who had nothing to give them even had he felt it was a part of his duties, the two men tramped out, muttering.

'What's the matter with them?' Ceci asked innocently.

'I wouldn't know.'

'When it comes to that, what's the matter with you? What are you doing still hanging around here?'

'Just watching things, like I was told to do.'

'Do you think that I might drown in my bathtub?' Cecelia asked with a smile that held no warmth. 'Get out of here, Hobie. Can't you tell when you're not wanted?'

Hobie only nodded and edged out into the hallway. He was not wanted, and he understood that. He also did not want to be there, but he was determined to do

43

the job handed to him as well as possible. He passed two young men with five-gallon buckets of hot water and an accompanying maid with a fresh towel and bath accessories. Cecelia was going to have a comfortable evening, at least. Hobie tried to remember the last time he had had a full bath. It had to have been before the first snowfall. While he was in Osborne, he considered, it might be a good opportunity to have a bath himself. Likely the boys from the trail drive were planning on getting drunk, shaved and bathed before they left town again. Why not him?

Where was Gene Brady? Could he still be at the doctor's? What was he doing, assisting in surgery? If Gene returned, Hobie himself would have a chance at taking a bath before supper. Walking back down the stairs to the hotel counter he signaled to the desk clerk.

'We need another room, for me and Miss Starr's other chaperon. Just put it all on the same bill,' Hobie said. He was a little surprised when the clerk did not so much as blink an eye at the request, but then everybody in the Basin knew that Gabe Starr was a wealthy man.

With the key in hand, he crossed the lobby again. As he passed the miners, he heard their sarcastic voices. '. . . The little girl's guard dog,' one of them said. Another answered, 'More like her little lap-dog.' Hobie glanced that way. The speaker, who had amused his three friends with the comment, was a bulky man, thick through the chest. He must have gone well over 250 pounds. His eyes were small, pig-like; his ears stood out a little from his blocky skull with the short-cropped hair covering it. His mouth was sagging, cruel. Hobie could see the man was primed for trouble. Probably he was drunk, perhaps bored with the inactivity as they waited for the mine bosses to arrive in Osborne.

'Come here, lapdog!' the big man called, but Hobie ignored him and proceeded up the stairs.

'Lapdogs don't have good hearing, Boomer,' another miner chipped in.

Hobie had good hearing, but he knew when to ignore things he heard. At five-foot-ten and around 160 pounds, Hobie was far from being a small man, but he knew better than to tangle with someone like this massive miner. None of the miner's weight would be flab. Men working in a hard-rock mine don't have the time to go soft.

The only way Hobie could stop a man like Boomer would be with a bullet, and he was not about to start shooting in this town – especially with the responsibility he had for Ceci's well-being.

Let the miners hoot and jeer. They would soon be gone from Osborne and Hobie would never see them again.

Now would be a good time to take his own bath, but he could not leave Ceci unwatched until Gene got back. Hobie's room was across from and one door away from Cecilia Starr's. He entered it and sat on the bed, leaving the door open enough so that he could keep an eye on Ceci's room. Hobie loosened his belt but did not remove his gunbelt or take off his boots. The precautions he was taking seemed unnecessary, but he had fixed in his memory the faces of Calvin Winslow and Gabe Starr when they warned him of what failure to protect the princess would mean.

Shifting the pillow to the foot of the bed, Hobie propped himself up so that he could continue to watch the hotel corridor. His eyes felt very heavy.

The voice awoke him from a doze he had fallen into.

'That all there is to this job?' Gene Brady said. 'Maybe it's not going to be as bad as I thought.'

'Didn't mean to drop off to sleep,' Hobie said, sitting up, rubbing his head, grinning sheepishly.

'Ceci still in her room?' Gene asked, winging his Stetson toward the other bed in the small room.

'She was taking a bath,' Hobie said.

'Oh,' Gene answered. Both men knew how long it might take a woman to bathe and arrange herself afterward.

'Then what?' Gene Brady asked.

Hobie stifled a yawn, 'She said something about going out to dinner.'

'I don't suppose we're invited.'

'Don't make jokes; I'm hungry.'

'So am I. I saw Pump Grissom, Trager, and a couple of the other boys over at this restaurant in the middle of town. Had a pile of potatoes and greens and what seemed to be slices of barbecued pork roast.'

'Why'd you have to tell me that?' Hobie grumbled. 'Don't you think you should take a turn watching the lady?'

'So you can go off and eat and leave me hungry?' Brady said. He was smiling good-naturedly as always, but he had a point.

'I was planning on getting a bath, too,' Hobie said.

'You made a lot of plans that depend on me doing your work, didn't you?' Gene said.

'I suppose I was just trying to make the best of the situation.' Ashamed of himself for only now remembering to enquire, Hobie asked, 'How's Randy getting along?'

'Doctor said he's seldom seen a gunshot that bad. Said he'd need to be a Chicago surgeon to patch that leg together properly, but had given it his best try.'

'Think he'll ever walk again?'

'Hell, the doctor couldn't guarantee that Randy will make it through the night.'

'Tough,' Hobie said, and then both men fell silent.

After a while, Gene Brady offered, 'One of us has to eat, Hobie. Why don't you go off first and fill your belly. I'll follow Ceci wherever she means to go. When you get back you can relieve me so that I can

47

take care of my own stomach.'

'Is that the way you want it?' Hobie asked hopefully.

Gene Brady laughed. 'No. Not much, but if we sit around here debating matters, neither of us is going to have his supper tonight.'

Hobie walked out into the cool of evening, feeling that a load had been lifted from his shoulders – however temporarily. The air was cool and clean, the town mostly quiet. There was some ruckus from one of the saloons along the street, but there always was in that sort of establishment. He hoped that it wasn't any of the SD boys causing it, but even that was none of his concern right now. He walked on, looking for a likely place to eat. A stagecoach rolled past. It was behind schedule, late, for drivers didn't like driving their teams after dark even on known roads. There was too much chance of injuring a horse or breaking an axle. Who, Hobie wondered, would take a stage to Osborne? He considered that it could be the long-expected mine bosses here to gather their crews before striking out toward the Knob country.

He passed a young couple walking arm and arm along the plankwalk, both dressed in their finery, both smiling, neither sparing a glance for the ragged cowboy as they eased past. Well, Hobie reflected with a grin, he wasn't worth sparing a glance at.

From somewhere he caught the unmistakable scent of corned beef and cabbage cooking. It jerked at his empty stomach and he started that way happily. Corned beef, cabbage and boiled potatoes struck him as an excellent meal to tuck inside himself.

Hobie crossed the street and was passing an alley when he heard a nasal voice saying dismally, 'I can't find it! Oh, Lord, I'm lost if I don't find it.'

Hobie glanced into the dark alley and considered ignoring the plea for help, if that was what it was, but halted and called out, 'Are you all right back there?'

'Oh, I'm . . . can you help me out, mister?'

'I'll try,' Hobie said, starting that way past a stack of empty wooden crates. 'What seems to be your problem, partner?'

'No problem,' a different voice responded. The voice belonged to no one Hobie knew, but somehow seemed familiar. When the three bulky shadows separated themselves from the darkness of the alley night, Hobie knew who it was and knew he had made a mistake.

Boomer, the silver miner, didn't even bother to speak before he took Hobie roughly by the collar and turned him, banging his back against the planking of a building. He smelled strongly of whiskey and the strength of his massive body was apparent. Hobie was held up against the side of the building as one of the other men lifted Hobie's Colt revolver from his holster.

'What's the trouble?' Hobie asked in a strangled voice, knowing there was no trouble except that

Boomer was a drunken bully. It's pointless to ask a logical question of such a man. Boomer felt like beating someone up, and he had selected Hobie.

'What are we going to do with the pup, Boomer?' the man holding Hobie's pistol asked. 'String him up? Gut him? Peel off his hide?'

'I don't know,' Boomer said with a sort of triumphant glee. 'I figure to just give him a few boxing lessons for now.'

The words were barely out of Boomer's mouth before the big man drove a fist into Hobie's belly, driving the air out of his lungs. Bending forward, Hobie was met by an upper-cutting fist which snapped his head back. Blood filled his mouth and bile flooded his stomach.

When Boomer released his grip on Hobie's collar, he found that his legs were rubbery. Hobie staggered forward, trying to duck away from the miner's fists, but he didn't have the speed to do it. A right-hand blow landing flush against his jaw rocked his head back again. An overhand left bounced off his forehead, starting tiny, brightly colored pinwheels spinning in his head.

'You're not teaching him right,' one of the other men said with a sharp snort. 'Look, he ain't learned a thing.'

'Some are slower than others,' Boomer said, and then he swung a punch that seemed to come up from his toes and land on Hobie's chin with the solid force of a sledgehammer meeting an anvil.

They might have hit him again; Hobie would never know. That last roundhouse right had extinguished the little pinwheels behind his eyes and drawn a black curtain across the world. Hobie fell without knowing it, sprawled against the oily earth of the dark alleyway.

Hobie awoke much later, feeling the chill of the evening first and then the savage ache of his stomach, jaw and shoulder. His face was pressed against the ground. He lifted his head to breathe and his head filled with thundering, thudding pain. Briefly he lay it back down against the cold earth. Then, minutes later, he tried to rise and found that his arms and legs refused to obey his fuddled brain's commands. He spent another few cold minutes waiting for his mind to clear, waiting for life to return to his seemingly dead limbs.

On his feet after long minutes of effort, Hobie spotted his Colt lying in the alley, picked out by a bit of glinting starlight. Brushing it off, he holstered his gun and staggered on drunkenly toward the head of the alley. He leaned for a moment against the side of the building, straightened his battered body and hobbled across the street toward the hotel, his hunger and other thoughts banished from his mind. He wanted only to find his bed, pull up a blanket and rest.

Hobie crossed the hotel lobby under the disapproving eyes of the clerk, who must have seen just another drunken cowboy staggering home. Achieving the staircase, Hobie made his way stiffly upward. If not for the banister, he might have fallen. Finally reaching the second-floor corridor he stumbled toward his room, bracing himself now and then against the wall. Panting, he entered his room. Gene Brady was not there. Why would he be? He would be watching the Lady Ceci wherever she had gone.

Hobie caught a glimpse of himself in the mirror, and weary as he was, as much as he longed for sleep, he took the time to wash his face, surveying his torn shirt and the marks on his face unhappily. He dabbed carefully at the blood crusted below his ear. There was an egg-sized lump on his forehead and his jaw was swollen and bruised. With the size and strength of Boomer, he thought he was fortunate that his jaw was not broken.

He had done a fair job of taking care of Cecilia Starr, but made a damned poor one of taking care of himself.

Taking a moment to dampen his head with water from the ewer, he carelessly brushed back his dark hair, dried his face and made his way heavily to the bed where he sat, head bowed, his entire body begging for relief.

The door opened and Hobie looked up, expecting to see Gene Brady. It was Pump Grissom. The red-bearded Pump had obviously been out drinking.

'Hello, kid!' Pump said, entering the room on

staggering legs. 'It looks like you've had a time for yourself, too. Where's Gene? I wanted to talk to him.'

'He's off somewhere watching Ceci,' Hobie said. His head continued to ache and throb. He didn't need a long conversation with an obviously drunk Pump Grissom just then.

'He is?' Grissom said in a slurred voice. He was holding on to the door jamb with one hand for balance. His eyes were red and vacant. 'Where would she be at this hour?'

'There's no telling. She wanted to go out to supper and then do some shopping – I suppose there are still a few shops open this time of night in a town the size of Osborne.'

'You do?' Pump asked, almost losing his grip and his balance. 'I wouldn't.' His badly focused eyes seemed to notice Hobie's condition for the first time. 'Hobie? What time do you think it is, at a rough guess?'

'I don't know,' Hobie said with some irritation. He only wanted to be left alone, to sleep. 'Maybe nine, ten o'clock.'

Pump Grissom leaned nearer, studying Hobie with drunken intentness. 'You been out drinkin', too?' Pump asked. 'You know me and Trager, Spuds McCain, we started early and ended late. I almost hate to tell you, but I will. The sun will be coming up in an hour or so, Hobie.

I went past Ceci's room on my way here. The door

was open and there was a maid in there cleaning up. Ceci wasn't there, so of course neither was Gene. Hell's fire, boy, don't tell me you've gone and lost both of them!'

FOUR

Hobie didn't answer Pump; he couldn't. In his way he was feeling as blurry as the drunken Grissom. It was no wonder that Hobie was feeling so stiff and cold. The last blow that Boomer had delivered to his head had knocked him unconscious and he had ended up sleeping the night away in the alley. Now as his mind finally started to clear, the waking world held too many questions and dark possibilities, much more serious ones than the corridors of night.

'Cecilia Starr is gone?' Hobie asked.

'Her and Gene Brady both, near as I can tell. Maybe they both got new rooms or moved to a different hotel for some reason, though that don't seem likely to me.'

'No,' Hobie agreed, 'it doesn't make sense to me either.'

'So – you figure someone jumped Gene and made off with the girl?' Pump asked, his red, drunken face growing somber.

'Someone like who?'

'Only name comes to mind is Hal Bassett,' Pump replied.

'Maybe she just felt like running off somewhere and Gene had to try to follow her,' Hobie said, not believing a word of his own conjecture.

'Maybe so,' Pump replied in that slurred voice. The man was obviously exhausted by liquor and lack of sleep.

'You'd better get off to bed,' Hobie said, rising from the bed – a movement that filled his head with a spark of fiery pain. He winced and waved a dismissive hand at Pump.

'You're right. I will, Hobie. I need to be in some kind of shape when we head back to the SD. But I'll be all right. As soon as I get out of sight of the next bottle. There's a bunch of us that are going to ride home hurting just a little. But, Hobie, just now I'd rather be in my boots than yours.'

Hobie only nodded as Pump slipped away toward his own bed. Grissom was right, he knew. The other boys were only going to be suffering a hangover. Hobie's position was much more dire. Through stupidity he had managed to lose Cecelia Starr. His excuse was a sound enough one, but would Gabe Starr even listen to any excuse before Hobie was fired and run off the SD?

'Gotta find. . . .' Hobie muttered through split

lips. He staggered toward the door, his mind filled with urgency, his body plagued with pain. Yes, he had to find Gene and Ceci, but where was he supposed to even start looking?

He wanted to find Calvin Winslow and confess, to ask for help. The foreman might be no more sympathetic than Gabe Starr would be, but he would be as frantic as Hobie himself was at the loss of the girl, and make every effort to help find her.

Wouldn't he?

Hobie did not even know where the SD foreman was at the moment. Likely sleeping, at this hour. And would Winslow be thrilled to wake up to a message like Hobie was carrying? Hobie was suddenly sapped of inertia. He was eager to go, to protect his job, the woman, to find Gene, who might have gotten himself into a real fix or be terribly hurt, but he was wading in treacle, both mentally and physically. He hadn't an idea in his head and his body felt too battered to respond to his suggestions.

What then? Something had to be done as soon as possible. Ceci might be riding away – or being spirited away, and the miles would be passing with each indecisive moment. When in doubt, make some move! With an effort Hobie managed to take his last clean shirt from his saddle-bags and shoulder into it. Starting at the only place he could think of, he walked stiffly downstairs through the cold, empty lobby and walked toward the desk clerk. This one was not the man he had seen the day before. Round, his sagging face set in what seemed to be a habitual scowl, he watched Hobie's halting approach with disapproval – another battered, drunken cowboy of which he had seen too many in his time as a night desk clerk. The man waited for Hobie to halt, lean heavily on the counter and speak.

'I'm looking for a woman,' Hobie said. His battered lips caused him to lisp slightly.

'You'd be better off catching up on your sleep,' the stout clerk said.

'Her name is Cecilia Starr,' Hobie persisted. 'Young, dark-haired, blue-eyed. She was in room number 16.'

'We don't give out information about any of our patrons,' the clerk said.

'No I know that.' Hobie was having trouble breathing. His ribs ached terribly. 'I just want to know if she's still here or if she checked out. The same for a man named Gene Brady – he was in room number 13. They're friends of mine and they seem to be missing.'

'Oh?' the clerk tried to assume a concerned expression, but he wasn't really interested in a wandering cowboy's problems. Or maybe his face was just not built for showing concern. He did try to answer politely. 'Look, mister, I just came on duty three hours ago. One man checked in; no one checked out. Are you sure your two friends didn't just decide to go away together?'

'No,' Hobie had to admit. 'No. I'm not. Thank you.'

Go off together? Gene didn't even like Ceci, and he was under the same obligation to Gabe Starr that Hobie was. Ceci was a clever girl, could she have somehow tricked Gene into taking her somewhere – to meet Hal Bassett, for example?

That made no sense. Gene was not stupid either. Gabe Starr would have his hide if such a thing was done. Then. . . .

Then what? Hobie had no ideas left. All he could think of doing was to try filling himself up with coffee and waiting for the other boys to start waking up; someone had to know where Calvin Winslow was. Hobie was counting on Winslow's understanding and advice. He was expecting a scolding, but then the SD foreman was bound to help, to suggest some course of action.

Outside the eastern sky was pink and rose, colorful drapes parting for the arrival of the sun. It was a little startling on this confused morning to realize that dawn was already breaking. There was a small restaurant one block along and across the street, and guided by the scent of fresh, strong coffee, Hobie made his way there.

The place was busy but not crowded. Waitresses in white dresses moved among the tables carrying gallon pots of coffee and platters of pancakes, wearing their weary-cheerful smiles. Hobie saw no one from the SD, but in one corner a group of miners, identifiable by their dress, sat eating. He scanned their faces, but Boomer was not among them, nor were his nameless pals from the night before. In another corner two men in gray town suits sat hunched over their coffee, their faces intent and eager. The newly arrived mine bosses? Hobie didn't know. They could be anybody.

A waitress approached his table, placed down a cup, filled it with rich dark coffee and asked what he'd have to eat. Hobie told her he'd have to think about it and she went away. Somehow the ravening hunger of the night before had dwindled although Hobie had not had a bite to eat. Without being aware of it, he found that he was rubbing his stomach, feeling the bruised ends of his lower ribs. Maybe Boomer had beaten the hunger out of him. Knowing he had to eat something, he asked the waitress for a short stack of pancakes when she returned to fill his coffee cup.

He ate slowly, sipped at his coffee, watched people come and go. There was no sign of Boomer and his pals, no appearance by the Starr-Diamond boys. It was bright, cool and clear when Hobie stepped outside again. The streets were beginning to be filled with the normal movements of people engaged in their various businesses.

Hobie stood on the plankwalk beneath the awning of the restaurant. He alone of all the people in

Osborne town had nothing to do, nowhere to go. Or rather, he had much more to do than almost any of them, but had no idea of how to go about things.

Across the street he saw a familiar face. Spuds McCain was looking at the window display of an emporium. Hobie started across the street, dodged a beer wagon and two horsemen, eager to catch up with Spuds, who was at least a familiar face and would have some understanding of what Hobie was suffering through. Spuds looked no less the worse for wear than Pump Grissom had. Spuds could not have been to sleep yet after his night sampling Osborne's finest beer and liquor. His round, heavy face was red, streaked with purple veins. His eyes were bloodshot, pouched and glassy. Hobie could understand why Gabe Starr had not wanted to trust the older hands to watch out for Ceci in town, but had Hobie done any better?

'Spuds, I'm glad to see you,' Hobie said, stepping up on to the plankwalk.

'Why, Hobie, boy! I'm right pleased to see you, too!' Spuds McCain said, staggering toward him. The whiskey on his breath was rank and sour. He placed both hands on Hobie's shoulders. 'I was looking for someone to join me. Trager, old Pump, Tully Sharpe – they all seem to have packed it in. These younger men, the ones we have these days, have got no stamina.'

'You're right,' Hobie agreed, since it seemed the

thing to do. 'Spuds, I need to find Calvin Winslow. Do you know where he is?'

'Winslow?' Spuds stroked his beard. 'No, he was around for the first couple of rounds, but then he slipped off somewhere. No stamina,' Spuds said with a wink.

'But where did he go? I know he's not at the hotel.'

'Hard to tell, Hobie. There are a lot of places for a man to sleep in this town if he's got a few dollars.' Spuds winked broadly again.

'I suppose,' Hobie said with deflating hopes.

'What's the matter, Hobie? Tell old Spuds what's happened. It can't be all that bad – unless you've gone and lost Ceci Starr.' Spuds chuckled, then he seemed to sober briefly. 'That's it, isn't it? You've gone and lost the girl!'

'Along with Gene Brady,' Hobie said, and he proceeded to tell Spuds all about it as they walked slowly up the street. 'And now I can't find Calvin Winslow to ask what we should do.'

'Probably he'd tell you to go off somewhere and hang yourself,' Spuds said grimly. 'I knew something like this was coming. You know what I think. . . ?'

'Yes, Spuds,' Hobie said, 'I know what you think.'

The White Wind, Fate, irresistible forces. Should he try explaining that to Gabe Starr?

'I thought,' Hobie speculated, 'that if I could find Winslow, we could gather the boys and make a search, or ride out after her if we find out she's fled to Hal Bassett.'

'Well,' Spuds said, as they stepped down off the plankwalk into an alley – Spuds tripping on the way down from the walk – 'that wouldn't be a bad idea, if we knew where the foreman was, and if we could find any men sober enough to make a search or ride out in pursuit, if we knew that the girl was gone at all, or which direction she might have gone.'

'You're a help,' Hobie said sourly.

'No, I'm not, and I know it,' Spuds said, stroking his chin in meditation. 'You think she's gone and Gene Brady has gone after her? How do you know we won't find Gene stuffed into some water barrel along the alley? Hold up!' Spuds said at Hobie's expression. He held up a hand. 'Listen, some miners jumped you in an alley, didn't they? Who says that someone didn't knock Gene over the head and make off with Ceci Starr?'

'But why would someone do that?' an exasperated Hobie asked.

'Why?' Spuds said. 'How much do you think Gabe Starr is worth?'

'Kidnapping for money?' Hobie asked, startled by the thought.

'It's been known to happen,' Spuds said.

Hobie moaned unhappily. 'If anyone's got her, it's Hal Bassett, and it's because she wanted to go with him,' Hobie guessed.

'And you think that Hal Bassett is above knocking Gene in the head and taking Ceci, who he assumes to be his woman, away.'

'Where would they go?' Hobie asked in frustration.

'Almost anywhere,' Spuds said. It was obvious to Hobie that Spuds had no more insights to offer and that he was just about out cold on his feet, his night's revelry catching up with him as the morning warmed.

They said goodbye, Spuds weaving his way toward the hotel as Hobie stood, hands on hips staring up and down the sun-bright street as if Ceci and Gene Brady might suddenly appear at his frantic wish. But they were not going to, he knew that.

Either Gene had followed her as she tried to escape, or something much worse had happened to him. Unless he was in on it and had run away with Ceci. That seemed the least likely possibility. What a couple they would make! The fresh-faced boy from Kansas and the lovely spitfire, Cecilia Starr. But you never knew; stranger things had happened.

Hal Bassett seemed the most likely culprit. It was known that the man was without conscience and that he had claimed Ceci for his own, mostly because he wanted the SD ranch – or so it was strongly suspected. Hobie walked aimlessly toward the stable where he had left his paint pony. He wanted to check on the animal since it seemed they might be having to ride in pursuit – or away in disgrace. Also, if Gene and Ceci had run away, they would have required horses. He could ask the stable manager. Not so if the miscreant were Hal Bassett – the bad man would have planned well enough ahead to have horses ready.

Maybe.

Or . . . a sudden thought jarred Hobie's sense of an orderly universe. No one had seen Calvin Winslow since last night. He was not in the hotel. He had just disappeared. What if Calvin Winslow, too, wanted to get his hands on the SD? It was a disloyal thought, but one worth examining. Winslow was trim, polite, undeniably handsome. Certainly he was the type who would appeal to Cecilia Starr more than a pup like Gene Brady. And when, eventually, she inherited the Starr-Diamond Ranch, she would need a capable foreman, a man who knew the range, the way the ranch was run. Who better than the man who held that position now?

It was all too much for Hobie to sift through at that moment, when his own battered body was complaining of lack of sleep. He had turned toward the stable when the girl perched on the edge of a loading dock called out to him.

'Hey there,' she said, 'looking for a job?'

'No,' he said, halting. 'I've got one.' For the time being.

The girl, no more than nineteen or twenty years

old, was wearing faded blue jeans and an Indian-decorated white blouse. She had a mass of untamed reddish hair and green eyes.

'What makes you ask?' Hobie said.

'Look at you!' The girl laughed in a way that Hobie could have objected to, yet amused him. She stood, hands on hips, surveying the tallish man with the bruised jaw, the lump on his forehead and the fresh dark scab of blood below his ear. 'I thought maybe someone had just fired you the hard way.'

'Not yet,' Hobie answered, because that was the likely outcome of his troubles.

'Well, if you need work sometime, come and see me. I've looked all around this town and there isn't much manpower available. I found a lot of drunken cowboys and a lot of men who looked like they didn't even know what the word "work" meant; there's not a lot to choose from.'

'Exactly what kind of workers are you looking for?' Hobie asked, extending the conversation not because he needed a job as yet, but because the girl was pleasant to look at and anything was a welcome distraction from his personal problems at the moment.

'The name is Trish Fisher,' the girl said, leaping down lightly from the loading dock to offer her small hand to Hobie. She was a head shorter than Hobie, and her smile was bright and captivating. 'I'm the camp manager up at the Wonder.'

'The Wonder?' Hobie repeated, perplexed.

'Sure. You haven't been around for long, have you? I mean the Wonder Mine, up at the Knob. We're the biggest silver producer in the territory. My uncle, Gus, was one of the original claimants to the Wonder. An old prospector who made good. He's retired now. He said it was because he was getting old, but I think it was just because he didn't want to deal with the day-to-day workings of an operating mine. He was happiest when he was just roaming the hills with his burro, which he still has, by the way.

'Uncle Gus lives in a big white house over in Laramie now. Making so much money a month that he can't even figure out how to spend it.'

'Sounds good,' Hobie commented.

'Well, you'd think so, but ask anyone who enjoyed his work and has lost it.'

'What about you?' Hobie asked Trish. 'Wouldn't you be happier in Laramie, wearing satin dresses and throwing yourself tea parties?'

Trish laughed. 'I was never invited to live there. I think Uncle Gus believes that a person who can make her way must try to make it on her own. That's the way I feel, anyway. It's true I have a job I cannot get fired from – thanks to Uncle Gus – but still I try to contribute to the world in my own small way.'

Trish continued, 'As for what kind of job I was

offering, it was camp dog – chopping wood for the fires, cleaning up after the miners, serving them meals when they come back up out of the hole in the ground which is Wonder. It's not glamorous, but it pays well. I was going to offer you three dollars a day if you were willing.'

'Three dollars!' He was making the standard dollar-a-day for cowhands right now. Top hands might make two dollars, but Hobie was not considered a top hand.

'I know it's not much,' Trish said. 'Our experienced hard-rock men, drillers and blasters, make five dollars a day, but their pay is recompense for the hazards of their daily work. Also, Mr—'

'Lee. Hobie Lee.'

'Also, Mr Hobie Lee, the Wonder Mine does not operate year-round. Hard winters and heavy snow make it impossible. So the pay isn't really as much as it seems.'

'I appreciate the offer,' Hobie said to the redhead. 'I'm just not in need right this minute. Besides,' he added with a frown, 'I'm not sure I could get along with mining men.'

'Oh?' Trish asked with a small frown of her own. 'Why do you think that?'

'I met up with a few of them in town, and their idea of fun seemed to be beating me up without cause.'

'Oh, that's where you got the lumps, is it? I'm sorry

68

– you don't happen to know who they were, do you?'

'I know who one of them was, a man called Boomer.'

'Boomer Haggerty, yes. He's a top powder man. I take it he was a little drunk?'

'He was.'

'That was it, then,' Trish said. 'The boys are mostly hard-working men, but when they hit the liquor, they don't know how to handle it. That and free time – when they're not working, they don't know what to do with themselves.'

'So they go around beating up strangers,' Hobie said acidly, because the girl did not seem to have much concern about what her men did off the job.

'I suppose so. I don't really know what they do when they're off the property. How would I? When the Wonder closes for the winter, I go back to Laramie. I have no idea where they go or what they do. It's a tough job, Hobie Lee, being trapped underground, not knowing if the mine will cave in at any minute, which dynamite charge will tear them apart. That and they never even know if there will be a job come spring. Schaefer and Suggs didn't even get into town until yesterday.'

Hobie nodded, remembering the two men he had seen whom he had taken for mine bosses.

'You see, no one ever knows when a mine might play out and you can't scrape enough silver for a dime out of it. When they leave they can only hope there's a job to return to. It can be a frustrating sort of life.'

'I get frustrated too,' Hobie said, 'yet I seldom go around looking for innocent people to beat up on.'

'Oh, I wasn't trying to stick up for Boomer, or the mine, just explaining. You've probably never been around that kind of man. I have, most of my life.' She shrugged and turned to look down the alley at a group of men passing as if they were potential workers.

'I can tell you've other things to do, Hobie,' Trish said. 'If it all goes wrong, come on out and see me at the Wonder.'

Again, she casually shook his hand and turned away. Hobie watched her walking in her jeans, her wild red hair blowing in the wind. How would that be for a boss? he asked himself, with a shake of his head. He didn't let himself ponder it for long; the lady was right – he had other things to attend to.

His paint pony had been groomed and fed, and it looked perky, its eyes bright with interest as Hobie visited it in the corral outside the stable. Inside the barn he talked to a gloomy man who had lost an eye and now sported a black patch.

'The wagon is still here,' he told Hobie. 'You can look out back and see it. The horses are in the corral with yours – you probably saw them. What I'd like to know, mister, is when someone is going back to claim them and pay their feed bill.'

'That'll be the SD foreman, Calvin Winslow. You must know him. You know the SD is good for any bill.'

'Sometimes it's better to have cash in hand than trust a rich man to do what's right,' the stableman said sourly.

'You know Gabe Starr's reputation, he isn't like that.'

'And he ain't here, neither. Maybe he don't worry about his cash, mister, but I have to.'

There's was nothing more for Hobie to say. He reclaimed his saddle and the paint pony, wishing he had enough cash in his pockets to pay the man on the spot, but he did not.

Where was Cal Winslow? The foreman should have been taking care of these matters. As Hobie should be taking care of Cecilia Starr. It seemed no one was seeing to his work as well as he should be.

Hobie rode his horse at a slow, plodding walk back uptown, his eyes hopefully searching everywhere for a sign of Ceci and Gene Brady, but in the pit of his stomach he already knew, believed, that they were long gone from Osborne. But where? And why?

Ceci had to have convinced Gene to take her somewhere. But how could she have done that? Dumb question – Ceci Starr was a beautiful woman, she could tie a pup like Gene Brady into all sorts of fancy knots.

Either that or someone had put Gene out of the

way through violent means. . . . Hobie saw Spuds
McCain sitting alone on a wooden bench in front of
the Golden West Saloon. He was dozing in the new
sunlight, a mug of beer in his hand. Hobie went that
way and swung down from his pony. Hearing his
boots on the plankwalk, Spuds opened his eyes and
tilted back his hat. Looking up at Hobie, Spuds
yawned and nodded.

'I hear you got some trouble,' Spuds said. He
briefly removed his hat to run his hand over his bald
head. He smiled, took a sip of beer and waited,
expecting an answer.

'You know I've got trouble. Who told you?'

'Pump Grissom.'

'What am I to do, Spuds? Have you seen Cal
Winslow? I hate to do it, but I'm going to have to tell
him the woman is gone.'

'No. I haven't seen him. It seems that Cal has more
friends in Osborne than any of us knew. I don't
expect we'll see him until tomorrow morning when
we ride out for the SD. That'll give the boys time to
sober up. A few of them tried to stand the town on its
head last night.'

'I know.' Hobie sagged on to the bench beside
Spuds. He drew his feet in as a pair of town ladies
walked past. 'Spuds? What am I to do? Do you think
maybe we could gather the boys and tell them,
spread out around town, looking for tracks, ride to
the outlying farms and ask if anyone's seen Ceci and

Gene Brady?'

'I don't think the boys, the shape they're in this morning, would be eager about doing that, Hobie. Besides, there isn't a chance of finding anyone who's seen 'em, not if they're trying not to be seen. And as for coming across the tracks of two unknown horses. . . .' Spuds made a puffing noise with his lips.

'No, sir, Hobie, my boy – they're gone, and you won't find them. You never should have let the girl out of your sight.'

Hobie didn't answer. He was too disgusted; the whole episode had made him sick. It was the end of his cowboying days on the SD and he knew it.

'Well,' Spuds said, taking another drink of beer, wiping his sleeve across his mouth, 'it was all pre- dictable, I guess. The White Wind is blowing pretty hard this spring.'

'Please, Spuds,' Hobie pleaded. He needed to hear no more of the man's nonsense, but Spuds was not to be silenced.

'Yes, my boy, the first time I heard it was late last week; since then I've been hearing it every night, a little louder, nearer. I knew it was warning me that we were heading into a tough year – I tried to warn all of you boys, don't you recall, Hobie?'

'I recall,' Hobie muttered. He was fingering the knot on his forehead. It was painful but the swelling seemed to have gone some.

'Yes, my boy. Every night. You'll hear it yourself

one of these nights when you're alone. A constant warning of trouble to come. A man who hasn't experienced it mocks me; those who have begin to hear it and to understand – that's why I was trying to tell you new, younger men about it.'

To change the subject, Hobie asked, 'Has anyone been to see Randy Dalton? I've been wondering how his leg was doing. I just haven't had the time to get to the doctor's to ask about him.'

'Barney Keyes went over there, but he was pretty drunk by the time he got there and the doctor wasn't real hospitable. Trager and Tully Sharpe are planning on going over there this morning.' Spuds finished his mug of beer and looked down at it regretfully. Hobie thought it was because he was at least making an attempt to get well, and had promised himself to cut down on his alcohol consumption today.

Hobie also realized that he was quite comfortable sitting on the bench in the warm sunshine, and that he was advancing his program to find Ceci and Gene Brady not at all. He rose and asked Spuds one last question:

'What about Hal Bassett?'

'What about him, Hobie?'

'I don't suppose anyone has seen him around town.'

'Nope,' Spuds wagged his head heavily. 'I don't suppose the skunk would be any more welcome here than he would be on the Starr-Diamond. I've been told that there are certain folks in this town who would like nothing more than to corner Hal Bassett in some dark alley. One thing about that, is that Hal used to ride for the SD, and now there are certain townspeople who don't like any SD cowboy.'

'Some of the miners?' Hobie asked, wondering if that was a part of the reason Boomer and his friends had beat him up.

'I didn't hear no names,' Spuds said. 'My only answer to your question is, I don't know. I doubt very much Hal Bassett would show his face in this town.'

So Cecilia Starr would have had to get someone to take her somewhere else to meet Hal. Hobie didn't know that, and he didn't know how she could have convinced Gene Brady to do such a thing, with Gene knowing that his job was at stake and that he was letting Hobie down as well.

The longer he thought about things, the less clear any of it became. It was time to follow the rule of uncertainty: when you aren't sure which move to make, do something!

FIVE

After leaving Spuds, Hobie walked his horse to the small restaurant up the block and took on fuel; he had a feeling he was going to be doing some riding. He had until the following morning to find the Starr woman and get her back to Osborne. After that, the game would be up. Calvin Winslow would know what had happened and so Gabe Starr would learn that his daughter had been lost. Hobie Lee, if he survived, would be free to ride the wide land again, looking for some kind of job to get him through the year, but Hobie did not want to leave the SD. Gene Starr had paid his men and fed them, given them a comfortable bunk throughout the long winter when they were doing no work at all. Another rancher might have cut them loose when the first snows fell, but Starr had treated his men with compassion, probably because he had lived through hard times himself in his early years.

Damn the girl!

After eating, Hobie stepped into leather once again and rode out of Osborne with no fixed plan in mind. The early sun which had cheered him not an hour before now became an annoyance, glaring into his eyes. Hobie supposed it was that way in so many cases – your mood could alter your perception of almost anything.

Halting at the town limits, Hobie paused to try to come up with something sensible – he couldn't ride the plains in a vague hope of finding them. Which direction would they have gone? North, south, west? Hobie's head was aching again. The knot on his forehead seeming to throb with his studied thinking.

Ahead he could see the sunlight glinting on the face of Corken Creek, the river they had crossed with the herd the day before; and it gave Hobie pause to think. The runaways would need water for their horses if they were traveling far. Would they follow the river? Who knew? Had their escape been a planned thing at all, or a sudden mad whim to which no real thought had been given?

Still with no plan himself, Hobie turned the paint northward, toward the Knob country. With luck he might be able to find signs of a recent passing in the mud along the creek. He knew that his plan, if it could be called that, was probably doomed to failure, but he had to do something! What else was there? To sit in his hotel room in Osborne and await his fate?

He rode on, following the meandering river. The sun was now on his back. He walked the paint along the river-bed, searching hopefully for the tracks of two horses crossing. He did find one place where someone had forded the river, but these were two heavy wagons, many horses and a group of men afoot. He lifted his eyes toward the bulk of the Knob. These were the tracks of the mine workers returning to their job site, a caravan he did not wish to follow.

Cottonwood trees were rife along the creek now. The town of Osborne was still in sight on his left, but it was a silent collection of matchbox-sized structures from here. Hobie rode on, disgusted with himself, mistrustful of his instincts.

Ahead of him in the shifting shade of the cotton-wood trees, Hobie saw an encampment of some kind, and a shrieking voice reached his ears. Frowning, Hobie slowed his horse and leaned down to peer through the trees. There was a group of boys playing along the river's edge. They had set up a lean-to of canvas and had a fire which was not lit just now. Hobie started the paint on again, thinking – kids see everything.

The boys stopped what they were doing, which seemed to be only wild horsing around, and stood facing the rider. They were a fairly ragged bunch, which figured – if they had Sunday go-to-meeting clothes they would not have brought them on a camping trip. They ranged from around ten years old to fourteen. Hobie didn't step from leather as he spoke to them.

'Hello, men. School out?'

'We got a holiday,' the oldest one said. He was dark-haired, dark-eyed and scowling. He waited for a further challenge, but Hobie could not have cared less if they were playing hooky. 'Nice set-up you have here,' he said, looking the camp over. It consisted only of the lean-to, a tarp propped up on a couple of sticks, and the fire ring. The youngest boy responded eagerly.

'We got our blankets in the tent, and I brought a big tin can to boil our beans in. We fish every day and bake them in the stones.'

'Seems like you have about all you could need,' Hobie said, smiling. 'Boys, I'm looking for some friends of mine. They might have come this way. It would have been late last night or early this morning – before the sun was up.'

'You don't mean that mob of miners?' the middle boy asked.

'No, this was a man and a woman. I don't know what horses they had.'

'I do,' the youngest one said, still eager.

'How could you know anything, Bucky?' the oldest boy demanded. 'We couldn't have seen nothing last night, mister, we was all sleeping.'

'I wasn't,' the kid named Bucky said. 'I got up sometime after midnight to . . . I got up about midnight and I seen these two horses approaching, The moon was up and I could make out that it was a red roan and a steel-dust.

'The man, he was riding the steel-dust. He was dressed for a cowboy and he had his hat tugged low so that I didn't get a look at his face.'

'The woman?' Hobie prodded. 'Was she young or old. Fat or thin? Could you tell?'

'I could tell,' Bucky answered. 'She looked like a woman on one of those circus posters.'

Hobie nodded; he had seen a few of those posters where a curvy woman in tights was always featured.

'So she was pretty, was she?' Hobie asked.

'Mister, she was the prettiest woman I ever seen.'

'You're dumb, Bucky,' the oldest boy said crossly. 'It was dark and you probably didn't see nothing but a couple of cows.'

'You're dumb, Jimmy!' Bucky shot back. 'I know what I saw.'

Hobie spoke up, interrupting their bickering before it could continue. 'So, which way did they go? Across the river, or were they following it?'

'Across.' The boy pointed. 'Just before they got to our camp, they turned their ponies' heads and splashed on across.'

'Can you show me their tracks?' Hobie asked, 'So that I'll know them if I see them again?'

'Don't do it, Bucky,' Jimmy warned. 'We don't know this man. He could be the law or someone chasing down runaways.'

80

'He'll find the tracks himself now that I told him,' Bucky said reasonably. Then eagerly he ran toward the riverbank and pointed out the fresh tracks left by two shod horses. Hobie nodded his thanks, flipped the kid a nickel and splashed across the sun-bright river himself.

On the far side of Corken Creek he located the fresh tracks easily in the soft soil beside the river. He followed them a way across a featureless meadow. They were riding straight and hard. Hobie could see that, at least for a while, they had lifted their ponies into a gallop by the length of the horses' strides.

After a while the land began to slope upward, meeting the verge of a pine forest. Beyond this stood the bald granite bulk of the Knob. The riders could not be headed there, could they? No, after another few miles their tracks began to tend eastward. Apparently they – Ceci – had been riding straight for the timber where they could lose any pursuit before striking out on a true trail.

To where? To meet with Hal Bassett? Hobie quit trying to out-think the girl. He had no idea what Ceci had in mind, nor why Gene Brady was letting himself be used in this way. The girl was wilful enough to have made her escape on her own, so why take Gene? Probably, he considered, she had not found a way to shake Gene and instead convinced him to ride with her.

None of that mattered. Ceci was going to go back

home. Hobie would see to it that she did.

He crossed a pine-stippled knoll 200-300 feet high. The horses he was pursuing had slowed, but their tracks, somewhat obscured by pine needles, were still easy to follow, as fresh as they were. Reaching the crest of the rise, Hobie looked down to see a road between where he sat his horse and the next row of rising hills.

The mine road, he thought. It had to be. Riding down the slope he halted the paint at the bottom. Yes, there were fresh wagon tracks cut into the red earth and many boot prints. The prints of the horses he had been following were overlaid by these, meaning Ceci and Gene had crossed the road before the men had started toward the mine. That fit with the assumptions he had made.

It was difficult to tell, but Hobie thought that the horses had also turned to use the road. A little way on he found a set of tracks clear enough to identify with certainty. The day was pleasant, if cool, and Hobie rode along, flanked by forested hills. The scent of the pine trees was heavy in the air. A pair of jaybirds squawked at him or at each other.

Ahead now, he saw that the road forked. A wooden plank with inexpert lettering on it stood at the junction. An arrow painted on the sign pointed to the left, in the direction of the Knob. The sign said, 'Wonder Mine'.

That prompted a thought of Trish Fisher, the little

redhead whose uncle owned at least a part of the
venture. She had a nice smile and. . . . Hobie shook
those thoughts away, and determined that the two
horses he wanted had taken the other fork in the
road, away from the Knob, and deeper into the
forested land. Above, mountains thrust their snow-
streaked peaks skyward. There were a few dark
clouds now gathered among these. Hobie hoped the
good weather would hold for at least a few days, until
this business had been completed. A heavy storm
could ruin his chances of finding Miss Cecilia Starr,
washing away tracks and obscuring the land surrounding him.

He rode on to the north, watching the clouds, the
tracks on the road, glancing occasionally at the pine
forest closing around him. He saw no movement;
heard no sound. As the road he was traveling began
to narrow down, passing between two rising bluffs, he
heard what he took for lightning crackling. Then the
sudden jolt of a bullet slamming into his back
tumbled him from his horse. The paint reared in
panic, trotted off a little way. Hobie lay still against
the cold earth, realizing that he had been ambushed.
By whom...? He thought no further about that or
anything but the wash of fiery pain that swept
through his body and the cool wind drifting past
him.

He was down; he was badly wounded. He tried to
roll over but found he could not. Now hot blood

trickled from his back and he clenched his teeth. He wanted to shout, to cry out, but there was no one to cry out to. Would his attacker come to finish him off? No matter; he could do nothing to stop him if he came.

The clouds had crept nearer and it became darker. They could not have cut off the sun that much, he thought. No the darkness was of a different source, and it slowly forced his mind into utter darkness, utter and complete. For a while, just before the darkness settled, he was aware of a strange sensation, a whispery, mocking thing. He knew what it was. Just for that brief second that it caressed his body with damp, scarred fingers. It smelled of mold and decay.

It was the White Wind returning for its final visit.

Hobie's eyes blinked open. It was damnably cold; that was what had awakened him. There was snow drifting down, and it was not melting as it touched his body. He knew he had to move or die, if not of his wound, then of exposure. That was more easily said than done. He tried to lift himself up with his arms. All that did was reignite the fiery pain in his back. His arms seemed unable to raise him. He simply lay down again, panting from what seemed a terrific effort. There was no hope for it: he was not going to make it. He looked around for his horse, but couldn't see it. Not that it mattered; he hadn't the strength to climb back into the saddle.

He closed his eyes and again returned to the dark void.

'Think he's dead?' a voice in the void asked.

'Poke him with a stick,' another muffled voice suggested.

Nobody did that, but two men approached him and rolled him over. They didn't do it roughly, but again Hobie's back spasmed with pain.

He was shocked awake and lay staring up at the sky where a few lazy snowflakes still fluttered down. The men were hunched over him, faces unfamiliar but concerned.

'He's not dead, but he's shot up pretty bad.'

'Nothing to do for it but get him back to the Wonder.'

'That'll take half the day,' the other complained.

'Yeah, well, it could be you the next time. You can't walk away from the man and let him die. Come on, let's see if he can maybe sit his pony if we help.'

Hoisted to his feet, Hobie was lifted and placed in his familiar saddle. Then the three began to ride. The entire trip was torment. Blood continued to leak from his wound. He drifted in and out of consciousness, his head rockong heavily from side to side, pulsing with its own unique thudding pain.

How long the ride took, Hobie could not say. It seemed an eternity before they reached their destination – the Wonder Mine. They lifted him from the saddle and one of them yelled to what might have been the mine office. Hobie tried to thank them, but his words emerged as a mumbled, strangled sound.

'Well, for God's sake,' a familiar voice said, 'Hobie Lee.' Hobie managed to squint through the slits of his eyelids and identify the speaker by her voice and the mass of tumbling red hair which framed her pretty face.

'Trish,' he murmured.

'Yes, it's me, Hobie Lee. What are you doing reporting for work in this condition?'

'You know him, Miss Fisher?' a man asked.

'Yes, I do. Take him over to my cottage – carefully! He's not a sack of potatoes.'

Maybe not, but that's what Hobie felt like – if he could be said to feel that good. Again the blackness closed around Hobie and the last he remembered of that night was the concerned smile on Trish's face as they placed him on a bed.

In the morning he awoke with the brilliant sun shining through a glass window into his eyes. He tried to roll away from its glare, but found that the movement was interrupted by a flash of pain. Sighing heavily, he settled back and tried to close his eyes more tightly. Something else was wrong. He itched and could not scratch it. Forcing his eyes open again he looked down to find that his chest was wrapped in a linen bandage, wound around him and over one arm, immobilizing it.

'I did a pretty good job, huh?' Trish Fisher said. She was sitting beside his bed in a blue upholstered chair.

'Dandy,' Hobie muttered unhappily. His head had begun to throb as soon as he awoke. His back and chest felt as if someone had run him through with a red-hot poker. 'Did it have to be so tight?'

'Yes,' Trish answered, rising to her feet. 'It's all that's holding you together right now. Your left arm had to be immobilized so that you wouldn't tear anything loose. That's the way it's done.' She bent over him, and Hobie Lee caught the scent of jasmine on her.

'Hurts a lot. Doesn't it?'

'Only when I'm awake.'

'I know. But, you can't sleep all the time. Do you want something to eat, Hobie Lee?'

'I'm not sure I could get anything down. Let's forget it for now.' He grimaced with pain as he said that. Concern returned to Trish's eyes.

'I'm afraid there's nothing to do about the pain except let time take its healing course. We do have some morphine tablets around. Some of the miners get fractured bones and worse down in the hole. We've had to take off a few legs and arms, and the morphine eases their pain.'

'I don't get any because I don't work for the Wonder?' Hobie said with some heat. Another bolt of crippling pain shot across his back and down to his waist. Trish Fisher was watching him, her face a mask of sadness.

'No, Hobie Lee, it isn't like that. Uncle Gus told me some terrible stories about morphine. They gave it to soldiers during the War Between the States – when they could obtain it. Men with terrible wounds. It helped them . . . for a while. Even after they were healed up, though, they had to have morphine. It drove them mad, the need for it. Uncle Gus told me that he witnessed one wild-eyed soldier kill his physician because the man wouldn't give him any more morphine. There's a devil in the dope, he said.

'No, Hobie, I wouldn't give you anything like that. When you're well again, I want you to be completely well.'

She took the pillow from behind his head and plumped it up.

'I guess I understand, but Lord, it does hurt, Trish.'

'I know it does. Whoever shot you was for sure trying to put you some place where there isn't any pain.'

'I know. I wonder who. . . ?'

'You have to try to get up on your feet as soon as you're ready. That lying around on your back is no good for you either,' Trish said, with a half smile. She wiped back a red curl of hair from her forehead.

'I know,' Hobie said. 'When I'm rested enough.'

'Hobie, how long do you think you've been asleep, or unconscious, whatever you want to call it?'

Hobie frowned. The girl was trying to tell him something. 'How long?' he asked. 'It seems like only through the night.'

'This is the third day,' Trish Fisher told him.

'It can't be!'

'It is. Believe me,' the girl said in all seriousness. Hobie turned this over in his mind, then smiled.

'You know what, Trish? In that case, I think I'd better try eating something.'

'That's a start,' she said, patting his knee. 'We'll talk about getting you up on your feet after you put something down.'

She went out and closed the door behind her quietly. Hobie lay in the bed in the sun-bright room which might as well have been a dark prison cell. He couldn't get up, he could barely move, and he had business to take care of. He had certainly lost his job on the SD by now. There was nothing to be done about that. But he could, with luck, find the man who had shot him down. There was even the long chance that he could find Cecilia Starr. It was unlikely, but not impossible that she was still in the area.

Even if his job was lost, Gabe Starr had entrusted him with his daughter, and Hobie had failed at that simple task. Maybe it wasn't his fault, but he had failed. Gabe deserved to have his daughter returned to him if it could be done.

As to who had shot him, Hobie was at a loss. Hal Bassett was the first name to come to mind. The rogue hand wouldn't want anyone tracking Ceci down. Why, then, hadn't he done away with Gene Brady along the trail?

Or had he?

If not, Gene had suffered some sort of brain fever and could still be riding with Ceci. Would Gene have fired a shot meant to kill at Hobie? Hobie had taken the young Kansan for a friend. Had he been that wrong about the cowboy's character?

Ceci herself might have shot him. Hobie didn't know Cecilia Starr that well. Was she that cold-blooded?

There was one other possibility, although he couldn't figure out how it would fit what he knew. He had never been able to find the SD foreman, Calvin Winslow, since Ceci had vanished. Was he tied up in this somehow? Winslow and the other men were likely back on the SD by now.

Others? How about one of the miners at Wonder? Had Boomer decided to let a rifle finish the work he had started with his fists? How would the bulky man have known Hobie was riding that way?

Pondering all of this in circular fashion, Hobie's headache was twice as bad by the time Trish Fisher returned with a plate of food for him.

'It's a puzzling world, Trish,' he said, accepting the tray. 'Puzzling and quite painful.'

SIX

It was not that morning but the next that Hobie Lee was ready to venture outside the cabin where he had been staying. On the earlier day he had gotten out of bed with Trish's help and been allowed – forced – to walk across the room and around it until he knew ever scar and knot in the pinewood floor. He had grumbled. Trish had been cheerful. When he slipped, she was there to catch him.

On the following morning Trish arrived early. 'Ready to get a little fresh air?' she asked.

'I don't know if I'm ready for it.'

'You can't stay in bed forever,' she said, flipping his blanket off.

He suddenly wondered, 'How's my paint pony?'

'Fine,' Trish answered. She helped him pull on his boots and stood to one side holding his jacket, which she threw across his shoulders. There was no way he was going to get it over his right arm.

Hobie found himself wondering if he was self-centered. Only now had he thought to ask about his horse. Similarly, he had never been to see Randy Dalton at the doctor's, or even asked about him except on rare occasions.

'There you go,' Trish said, taking his hand to lead him to the door. As soon as this was swung open, Hobie's ears were assaulted by all the sounds of a working mine. Men shouted, mules passed by towing heavy carts. Somewhere a load of ore was being funneled down an iron chute. The sky was high and blue with only a few widely scattered white clouds riding the cold wind eastward.

'Where are we going?' Hobie asked.

'Nowhere, anywhere. I just wanted you up and moving,' Trish answered. 'Do you want to see the office?'

Hobie shrugged. It didn't matter to him at all. As they walked toward the mine office, a white building with a low green roof, Hobie let his eyes continue to rove the yard. He was looking for someone he hoped not to see again – Boomer, the savage powder man of Wonder Mine.

'Come on,' Trish encouraged as they reached the three steps leading up to the mine office door.

Hobie took in a deep breath as he gripped the rail beside the steps. Those three tiny steps seemed to present an enormous task.

'Let's go,' Trish said. 'Before you were sick, I bet

you'd have vaulted those steps in one leap. Let's get you well again – a step at a time.'

Gritting his teeth, Hobie stepped up and forward to reach the porch. Trish took him by the arm and led him in to the building where three men in shirts and ties worked. Two of them wore gray coats. The third was in shirtsleeves, a glass of some kind – like a jeweler's loupe – to his eye. He turned a small bluish rock one way and then the other and scribbled something down in the ledger on his desktop.

The other two men had been talking, pointing at a schematic map pinned to the wall, when they entered. Now they fell silent and turned to look at Trish and Hobie. Hobie decided that the map, with shafts and vaults drawn on it in blue ink, was a map of the Wonder's underground works.

'Well, Patricia,' the larger of the two men said, 'I see you brought your patient with you. Does that mean he's ready to go to work?'

'Maybe in a day or two,' Trish said with a smile.

This man Hobie liked at first sight. He was tall, heavy, had a pot belly and thin dark hair brushed straight back. The smaller, thinner man had not smiled and seemed to be annoyed at the presence of either Trish, or Hobie, or both. He had a sharp narrow face with foxy dark eyes.

'The name's Tyrone Schaeffer,' the big man said, stepping nearer to shake hands with Hobie. 'That's Walter Suggs.' He nodded at the fox-like man. 'The youngster over at the desk is Allen Pierce, the only one who does any real work in here.' Pierce, who was close to seventy years old, white-haired, wearing wire-framed spectacles, turned from his ledger to smile and nod.

A man entered the office without knocking, a young, broad man with an Irish face. He was carrying a bucket full of rocks. 'Brought these up from shaft three,' the man said in a thick brogue. 'Fresh litter for ye.'

'Thanks, Mac,' Pierce said, and the bucket was placed on his desk. The other two mine bosses crossed the room and crowded around the assayer.

'How does it look, Pierce?' Schaeffer asked, hopefully. 'High-grade, is it?'

'Seen worse, seen better,' Pierce answered in a dry voice.

Trish nudged Hobie toward the door. 'Let's go,' she said in a low voice. 'They've got eyes only for the rocks now.'

Once outside on the porch again, Hobie asked, 'That was silver ore?'

'Nothing else. What did you expect it to look like?'

'I don't know. Something like gold when you find it, all shiny and bright.'

Trish laughed. 'It takes a little more work for the silver to shine. It has to be refined, and it's a difficult process. Silver nuggets are found here and there, but they're unusual.'

'So,' Hobie asked, feeling ignorant, 'you don't worry about hold-up men lying in wait for your ore wagons?'

'Not unless it's someone with an ore-crusher and a smelter at hand, and there aren't many of those around. We take the ore to be refined in Denver and let the people at the mint worry about any robberies after they've coined it.'

'Even they don't have that much of a problem with it, do they?'

'Not with the weight of silver relative to its worth. The smart thieves go after gold and currency – that is, if there is such a thing as a smart thief.'

They started down the steps again and, reaching the bottom one, Hobie felt his boot slip and he started to slide. Trish grabbed him beneath his arms and steadied him. It was at that moment that three men walked past.

One of them was Boomer.

'The man's plain tuckered out,' one of his friends said.

'It's hard work being a professional lapdog,' Boomer said. 'And look who he's got now! I wonder what he's got that I don't?'

'Manners for one thing,' Trish said angrily. 'But you've at least got a job – for now,' she added. Boomer and his friends pulled in their horns. They didn't come all this way only to be fired their first week on the job. Hobie didn't know how much power Trish actually wielded around the Wonder, but it was obviously enough to send the miners off without so much as a sullen back glance.

'What was that about a lapdog?' Trish asked, as they walked back toward the cottage.

'I'll tell you sometime,' Hobie said. He had no wish to start discussing Ceci Starr just then. After another few yards he asked, 'Where are my guns, Trish?'

'In safe keeping. Why? Do you feel like shooting someone?'

'I'd feel better with my belt gun on around men like Boomer.'

She shook her head. 'We don't allow our men to carry guns or have liquor on the Wonder. We've had a few incidents in the past.'

Hobie understood, but he told her, 'Boomer won't let up on me, ever. I don't know what planted the seed in his mind that I deserved his hatred, but hate me he does. With only my fists I wouldn't stand a chance against him. I've got enough sense to know when I'm overmatched.'

'I won't let a fist fight start either. Especially with you. Look at you! You're not even half a man again yet.'

'Having my Colt on my hip would go a long way toward fixing that,' Hobie said.

'Having me on your side will do more,' Trish said, and she looked up at him with sparkling green eyes and a serious frown which became a serious smile. 'Do you want to see your horse?' she asked brightly, looking away.

'I'd better. I'd hate to have another friend feel that I've deserted him.'

Trish didn't ask him to explain that comment; instead, still holding his arm, she turned him toward the corral which lay behind the office in the cool shade of a stand of oak trees. There were more mules than horses in the pen, but the paint was there, munching hay. Hobie whistled and the horse looked up and walked toward him.

Hobie stroked its muzzle and said, 'I know you want to be moving. So do I.'

'You'll be leaving when you're able?' Trish asked, watching man and horse.

'Just as soon as I can,' Hobie said firmly.

Trish's voice was lowered as she asked, 'No chance of making a mining man out of you?'

'None in the world,' Hobie answered immediately. When he looked down, Trish had turned her face away. What in the world was the woman thinking? Make a miner of him? Then slowly an understanding of the meaning of her question came to him. Knowing what a woman was thinking had never been one of his strong points. Maybe it was all his imagination, but as they turned to return to the cottage, he noticed that Trish remained silent, her eyes turned down; and there was no more conversation.

Within a week Hobie was feeling well enough to rise, wash, dress, eat a good breakfast and walk around the Wonder by himself. He got some dirty looks from some of the miners who considered him an outsider and a lazy one at that. Fortunately, he did not encounter Boomer or any of his friends.

Hobie had finished seeing to his horse when he noticed Trish sitting on a low, flat boulder near the corral. The sun on this morning beamed through the branches of the trees, casting her into bright relief. It was only about ten o'clock so, as Hobie strode that way, he teased her. 'It must be nice not to have to worry about being fired.' He seated himself beside her on the rock, removed his hat and wiped his forehead on the cuff of his sleeve.

'I suppose.' Trish answered. She had her knees drawn up, her hands between them. 'I'm going to have to put you to work pretty soon, though, or I'll start hearing about it.'

Hobie laughed. 'Don't worry about me. I'll soon be gone. There's no work around here I'd care for.'

'No, I suppose not,' she said. A long silence followed. She was not looking at his eyes. Hobie tried to restart the conversation.

'I guess you plan on coming back here year after year forever.'

'I don't know – not forever, certainly. Mines play out, Hobie, and from what I see and hear, Wonder is in its decline now. When we're no longer hauling enough ore to pay our expenses, well' – she shrugged – 'Wonder will just be another of those old abandoned mines that clutter the landscape.'

'Then what would you do? If that happened? Go back to Laramie?'

'Probably. The mine might be leased out to some shoestring operators, but they wouldn't have any use for me here. As little as you have seen me doing, I like to think that I contribute, and I wouldn't if that proves to be the case. I like to feel needed, don't you?'

'Sure,' Hobie answered. 'But if you aren't working here, if you go back to Laramie, what would you do?'

'I haven't thought about it enough. I suppose I'd start a little shop. I don't really know.'

'You have the money for something like that?'

'Uncle Gus does. And I do get a small percentage of the mine profits. Yes, I have enough for something like that. I just don't know if I'd care for it. I've always been sort of an outdoors girl. What about you, Hobie? What would you like to do?'

'Like most every cowboy you'll ever meet, I'd like to have my own ranch. It wouldn't have to be a large spread; it would just have to be mine.'

'You like that work so much?'

'Yes, I do. There's no four walls around you when you're working cattle.'

'And that's important?'

'It's important,' Hobie said. 'Of course, now I don't even know when I'll have a job again.'

'Then you're sure that you're finished on the Starr-Diamond.'

'I'm sure. I've told you all about it before.' And he had. They had spent much time together over the past days, even sitting up past sundown, gabbing away about nothing a lot of the time. At other times their conversation turned serious and Hobie had recounted all of his problems since being told to watch out for Ceci Starr. Trish had understood, or pretended to, which is the same thing.

'Then what are you going to do, Hobie?' Trish asked him now. 'It makes no sense for you to try to track down Cecilia when the effort won't be appreciated, even if you are successful. Especially not by her! If she was willing to go to those lengths to get away from the SD, what makes you think she'd be willing to return with you?'

'I don't know.' Hobie shook his head and then brightened. 'I might just have to hog-tie her and throw her over her horse.'

'I can't see that working,' Trish said with a faint smile. 'Besides, Hobie, even if you got her back to her father somehow, she could give him any sort of wild story she can come up with – blame you for kidnapping her, maybe.'

'Nobody would – oh, yes, she might at that,' he had to admit. 'No matter, I was in charge of watching over her and I didn't do the job. I'll find her or die trying.'

'That seems a distinct possibility,' Trish said. 'Look at what's already happened to you. Is there any reason to believe they wouldn't try shooting you again?'

'None,' Hobie said after a moment's unhappy reflection. 'I'd like to find out who was responsible for that as well. I have a score to settle with the back-shooter.'

Trish was silent again. Hobie thought that the girl was going to try talking him out of the mad pursuit, encourage him to stay on at the Wonder. But there was no way that could be done. It would mean working day in and day out while the object of his quest got farther and farther away. Knowing that would eat away at him.

'When are you going to leave?' she asked.

'Tomorrow or the next day. It depends on how I feel when I get up in the morning. I think it will be tomorrow, Trish.'

'I'll see to it that you have your guns back,' Trish said, slipping from the rock. She walked off through the mottled shadows without a backward glance.

Hobie watched her go. The only friend he had left in the world, probably. The only woman who... Hobie slipped from the rock himself and began an aimless walk around the camp.

When the sun was just a dull promise in the sky the following morning, Hobie swung his feet from his bed and sat up, rubbing his head. There was a twinge of pain in his back, but Hobie judged himself well enough to travel, even though he had no idea yet where he was traveling or how long the trail would prove to be.

It was a fool's quest, he knew, but then Hobie Lee decided he was a fool. Nothing in his life had proved different. Look at him now – riding away from the pretty little red-headed girl. And a rich girl at that! Still, Hobie knew in his heart that he would never be satisfied with himself until he had reached the end of this personal road.

His rifle, he saw, as his eyes cleared of sleep, was laid on the bedside table. His gunbelt and holster containing his Colt .44 had been hung on the post of the bed's headboard. Trish had been there, then, while he was asleep.

As the morning brightened, Trish did not return to say goodbye. Hobie was not sure if that relieved or saddened him. Well, she had already said her goodbye while he slept, it seemed. Maybe that was enough for her.

Near the door Hobie found one more item that Trish had left him. It was a canvas sack, and when he peered in he saw a sack of dried pinto beans, a smaller one of coffee and an inches-thick slice of cross-cut ham. There were other items as well, but Hobie didn't sort them all out. It was enough food to see him on his way along the trail for at least a few days. After that, well, he had better come across some small settlement. He was trusting that Ceci Starr was bright enough not to have just ridden off into the wilderness with no destination in mind.

If only he was able to find her direction.

That was a rather gloomy thought. He knew where to start, of course, back on the east fork of the road where he had been ambushed. There would be nothing left of their tracks by now. He had to trust to luck, which, he reflected, had not been going his way lately. The White Wind, it seemed, was daunting his every move.

Maybe old Spuds McCain wasn't as crazy as everyone thought.

Hobie pulled his hat down, stepped out into the cool, bright sunlight and stood with the canvas sack in his hand, looking across the mine yard. There was no sign of Trish. He thought briefly of going to the mine office to look for her and say goodbye, but it seemed that she would rather have things this way.

Taking a deep breath, then, Hobie Lee strode toward the corral where his paint pony would be ready and eager to hit the trail. A blind trail leading . . . nowhere.

SEVEN

It took Hobie less than an hour to saddle and arrive at the point where the mine road forked. The cold wind gusted as he looked eastward, toward the fork that led deeper into the forested hills. The last time he had attempted to follow that trail, it had cost him. But the shooter, whoever he was, would be long gone by now. Besides, there was no reason to believe that a sane man would try to ride this unwelcome trail again.

Heeling the paint lightly, Hobie started along. An involuntary shudder passed through him as he rode past the point between two rising, pine-clad bluffs where he had been tagged by the bullet. This time, however, all was silence. There was only the wind rustling in the pines, the steady muffled clop of the paint's hoofs.

On the far side of the pass, the trail continued to rise into the hills. It grew narrower. Whoever lived

out here, used this road, would not need a way wide
enough for ore wagons as Wonder Mine did. Lifting
his eyes to the pale sky, Hobie saw a flock of crows, a
dozen of them, circling and cawing, wheeling in a
seemingly aimless sky-ritual. Beyond the hills, the
snow-streaked mountains stood implacably. These
were impervious to and uninterested in all of the
troubles and aspirations of men. They would be
standing there, huddled together in cold conference
long after the last man had played out his last folly.

Around noon, Hobie drew his horse into the trees
to let it graze on the new grass there, and he himself
broke into the provision sack to make a simple, ful-
filling meal of two slices of ham and some salt
biscuits, washed down with cool spring water. It
would do. The paint was having to scrounge for its
meal. The bright new grass was still short among the
pines. Hobie decided to give it a little more time. He
rose, stretched and looked northward, hoping, but
not expecting, to see some sort of ranch or town. He
saw nothing.

And then he did. A rider was approaching him
from the north, following the trail Hobie was using.
All right, then. Here came a man who could tell him
what lay at the end of the trail. Hobie tightened his
cinches and swung aboard, riding to meet the
stranger.

Hobie waited on the side of the hill, just inside the
forest verge. He wanted to have a closer look at the

rider before the man below spotted him, As the stranger rounded a bend in the road and continued toward Hobie, he could see that the man wore no hat. Odd. Then Hobie was able to recognize the reason for this. The stranger's head was swathed in bandages. He rode slightly slumped forward in the saddle of the steel-dust horse he straddled. Why did the horse seem important?

Then Hobie remembered, and he started forward down the slope. He could now see the man's face. It was dismal, bruised, but still recognizable.

'Gene!' Hobie called out, and the rider's head snapped up. He drew back the reins of the steel-dust and the horse slowed to a halt. Hobie rode forward cautiously, Gene Brady staring numbly at him. Hobie drew his horse up alongside Gene's.

The kid said miserably, 'Hello, Hobie,' and his eyes sloped away from Hobie Lee's gaze.

'Hello yourself, and just where in hell have you been, Gene? And why?'

The kid from Kansas mumbled his answer. 'I've been upcountry, there,' he said, nodding his head somewhere toward the north.

'All right. More directly, where is Cecilia, and why did you take off with her in the first place?'

'Last I seen of her, she was up in Lassen. It's a little town about a day's ride from here.'

'And you two thought you'd go up there to see the sights, leaving me in Gabe Starr's outhouse.'

'It wasn't that way, Hobie. I knew what we were doing to you. There was just no help for it. Ceci wanted to get up to Lassen, and I had to help her.'

'You had to help her,' Hobie said in a flat voice. His anger was barely contained. 'Why did you have to help her, and desert your partner?'

Gene Brady's face went pink beneath his sickbed pallor. 'You don't understand, Hobie. I took her out to dinner, you see. And when we were finished there, she kissed me, Hobie! She kissed me right on the mouth! My knees went kinda weak. I didn't have a chance. . . .' Gene's voice trailed away and Hobie Lee sat his impatient horse, glaring at the kid in disgust.

'It doesn't matter now, I suppose,' Hobie finally said. 'How could you let a woman trick you that way?'

'Right on the mouth, Hobie – you've got to understand,' Gene pleaded.

'Oh, I understand,' Hobie said furiously. 'I just thought that not even a corn-fed yokel like you could be so dumb as to fall for it, and leave his partner in a jam like you did.'

'I didn't think. . . .' Gene said pathetically.

'You've made that clear enough, Gene. Tell me this, did you take a shot at me?'

'At you!' Gene seemed completely shocked by the question. 'Of course not, Hobie. I'd never do a thing like that.'

'I thought maybe you got another kiss and decided to ambush me for her.'

'Hobie, please. I feel bad enough.'

'It's nothing you don't deserve.' Hobie breathed in slowly, deeply. When he felt a little calmer, he asked, 'All right, Gene, tell me what happened to you. And where is Ceci?'

'You don't want to go after her, Hobie.'

'You're right – I don't want to – but I am. Why don't you answer my questions?'

'I'll tell you about it, Hobie. Is it all right if we swing down? I've been in the saddle since sun up.'

'Let's do that, then, if it will make it any easier for you to talk to me.'

The two men swung down from their saddles and walked to a smoothed portion of the bank beside the road. They sat in the shade there; Gene groaned as he lowered himself. The man was hurting, no doubt about it, but Hobie was too angry to feel any compassion for the battered cowboy.

'What happened to you?' Hobie asked, and Gene glanced at Hobie with sorrowful hound eyes.

'It was up in Lassen. I tried to get Ceci back.'

'A little too late, weren't you? Who were you trying to get her back from?'

'Those men who were holding her. They said they were riding with Hal Bassett – I don't know – but Ceci didn't believe them. Where was Hal, then? she kept asking. No one gave her a straight answer. After a while she began to think that these men were kidnappers who knew who she was somehow. Maybe

from something Bassett had said, when he was brag-
ging. About how pretty she was, and how her father
owned a rich ranch down south. Maybe not... All I
know is that Ceci wanted away from them and asked
me to help her.'

'Did she ask with a kiss?' Hobie asked with some
sarcasm.

'You don't know how it was, Hobie. But I knew
then that Ceci was in real trouble, and I had taken
her into it. I felt responsible, and I guess I was. I
decided that I was going to get her and bring her
home.'

'Again – just a little too late,' Hobie commented.

'I know, Hobie! You can quit rubbing my nose in
it.'

'You said they were holding her. Where was this?'

'On a truck farm just outside of town. I got the
idea that one of the men—'

'How many?' Hobie asked.

'Four that I know of, there might have been more
involved. I got the feeling that one of them owned
the place, or was related to someone who did,
because they just moved into the house like they
lived there.'

'Where were you while this was happening?'

'Oh, I was right along. You see, at first Ceci
thought we were going to meet up with Hal Bassett,
so I kind of naturally rode along with the bunch.'

'You wanted to meet Hal Bassett?'

'Well, in a way, yes. I wanted to see what kind of man he was. Find out if he was good enough for Ceci, because if he wasn't I meant to plead my own case.'

'By then you wanted her?'

'I always wanted her, Hobie,' Gene Brady said earnestly. 'It's just that I know I have nothing to offer.'

'And now you have? Or did you figure that she had enough money for both of you?'

'You just aren't going to let up on me, are you, Hobie?' Gene Brady hung his head for a while, his hands clenched together. When he looked up, it was to say, 'I'd at least have always been good to her, Hobie. From what I have heard about Bassett...' The man shook his bandaged head heavily.

Hobie just stared at the kid. No, Gene knew nothing about women – even less than Hobie did. How often did they choose a handsome reckless man over a steady, honest one? Too often.

'Did Bassett ever show?' Hobie asked.

'No, he didn't, and that's just the point, Hobie. At first they told us that Bassett would be there in the morning. Then they said, well, he must have been delayed. After three days, Ceci began to get nervous, frightened of the men. They wouldn't let us go into Lassen, said she might miss Hal Bassett; besides they had everything she could want right there. Ceci came up to me one evening as the sun was going down. She came real close, and I could see that she was trembling. She said I had to get her out of there; something was wrong with that bunch. She thought maybe they were using her as bait to lure Hal Bassett into a trap.'

'Bassett is on the run, then?'

'From what I understand he's on the run from both the law and some past unsavory associates – why, I don't know.' Gene Brady looked into the distance. 'These men didn't strike me as lawmen, Hobie. Who knew what they were or what they would do to Ceci?'

'So you decided to take a try at getting the woman out. What happened?'

Gene Brady told him, 'The following morning I was up before dawn and I slipped out of the house to saddle our two horses.'

'And they were watching?'

'Of course they were. I should have known better, realized that men like them are always going to be watching, especially when they might lose something that's valuable to them.'

'What did they do?'

'What didn't they do?' Gene Brady asked, managing a tight laugh. 'Two of them jumped me in the darkness. One slipped my gun from my holster; the other had an ax handle, or something like it, and he tried to bash my head in. When I went down on my knees, both of them started trying to kick me to death. I think they would have, but their leader – a man named Casey – called them off. He bent down and told me:

' "You've got one chance to live, boy. You can get on your horse and ride as far as it will carry you without looking back, or we'll start digging your grave right now." '

'You got on your horse,' Hobie said.

'Yes, I did. I thought I caught a glimpse of Ceci watching from her window as I left, but that was all the looking back I did. I just rode on, feeling like the world's worst coward.'

'There probably wasn't another way. How'd you get your head bandaged?'

'I stopped at a creek to water my horse. I was bleeding bad from a split scalp, so bad that I could barely see for it dripping into my eyes. I got down from the gray, feeling like I was being watched, not caring. If they had followed after to kill me, I just didn't care any more.

'Anyway, I met this scrawny old whiskered man. He was panning for gold along the creek. I asked him was he having any luck, and he says no, but more than I was having, it seemed. He was a friendly old cuss. Funny, I can't remember his name just now, or maybe he never offered it to me. I wasn't thinking straight by then.

'The man offered me coffee and pancakes, and I took him up on it He washed my head and face off with hot water from his fire, then tore a cloth into strips and bandaged my skull for me. I ate what he

113

offered then fell asleep for a while. When I woke up again, it was nearly dark and the old man was gone.'

'He probably didn't want to get involved in whatever trouble you were in,' Hobie said.

'That's probably it,' Gene agreed. 'Anyway, I spent the night there. The old man had left me with a blanket. Come morning, I started on my way again.'

Hobie found that for some reason his anger against Gene Brady was fading. Not enough for him to pity the battered cowboy, but some.

'What are you going to do now, Gene?' Hobie asked. A sad, crooked smile curled Gene's mouth.

'What is there to do? I can't go back to the SD, that's obvious.'

'There's a mine not far from here where you could maybe get hired on.'

Gene shook his head. 'Why would they? I'm not able to work the way I am, Hobie. No, but I do have an idea I might follow through on. I'll bet Randy Dalton is still abed down in Osborne, as bad as his leg was shattered. I thought I might go to see him; maybe the two of us can find work swamping out saloons or cleaning up the stables. I don't dare return to the SD, and it seems that Randy won't ever be able to climb into leather again. It would be something; we could get along, find some way to make a living.'

Hobie nodded, reflecting on how low Gene's expectations for himself had fallen since he came West.

And wasn't Hobie in the same situation himself? Yes, as he had thought before, it was a puzzling and painful world. There was the brief thought that he should offer to let Gene ride along with him, but that would be leading him back into the same trouble he had just run away from.

Hobie rose and dusted off his hands.

'Maybe you'd better give me the names of the men who are holding Ceci,' Hobie said.

'I don't know them all,' Gene said, wincing as he rose. 'There was Casey – the leader, I think. And a fat man named Turk. Another man I heard them call Arnie. He wears a black walrus mustache and has cold little eyes. Even if you'd never met him you'd know on sight that he was trouble. I never caught the other man's name. All I could tell you is that he was up from Texas – I know the drawl.'

'And none of them ever mentioned Hal Bassett again after they took you to the farmhouse?'

'Not unless Ceci demanded to know something directly. Then they seemed either to know nothing or to be lying about it.'

'All right,' Hobie said with a dissatisfied sigh. 'Give me the best idea you can on where to find the farm.'

'You're still going after her?' Gene asked with surprise. 'Even after what I told you about the situation?'

'I'm still going,' Hobie said. 'Maybe I can't manage things any better than you did, but I have to try – it's my job.'

The last bit of this shamed Gene again evidently, but he crouched to sketch a rough map of the town of Lassen and the road leading toward the farmhouse, as Hobie had asked. They parted without words of farewell, without good wishes for the future. Simply as two men who have had a chance encounter along the trail and must ride on in different directions, toward different objectives.

And, after all, that was all that their meeting had been.

Sunset was coloring the western sky when Hobie Lee reached the tiny mountain town called Lassen. It seemed out of place, like a lost traveler. Why had it been built here in the shadow of the mountains, and how long could it possibly endure?

The town was quiet – there wasn't enough population for it to get boisterous, it seemed. Hobie knew, from Gene Brady's account, that it could be a dangerous place anyway. In a small rural place like Lassen, every stranger was immediate cause for speculation. A lone rider appearing from nowhere, arriving at a place he had no business being, was rare enough that word of his arrival would not take long in being mentioned around. He walked his weary paint slowly up the street.

On his left he saw a small building, brightly lighted, which was too small to be considered a saloon, but seemed to serve that purpose for the men of Lassen. There was the rumble of conversation inside and once the clinking of glasses. On the porch in front three men stood passing a pint bottle of whiskey around. These looked up at the unfamiliar horse and unknown rider.

'Evenin', friends,' Hobie said. 'Can anyone tell me where I might find somewhere to spend the night in this town? I was just passing by and thought it might do me some good to sleep in an actual bed for a change.'

'Where are you from?' one of them asked truculently. The man was half-drunk, it seemed, and probably meant nothing by his challenge.

'I just got fired down at the Wonder Mine,' Hobie improvised, 'and decided to make my way home to Wyoming.'

'What'd they fire you for?' a second man asked.

'Just over a difference I had with the boss,' Hobie replied, tilting his hat back.

'I know all about that,' the third man piped up. 'I once got me a job down there over the summer. It didn't agree with me.'

'Work don't agree with you, Cappie!' the drunken man gibed.

'Well, there's that, too,' the man called Cappie agreed with a grin. 'Tell you what, mister,' he said to Hobie, 'there's a widow lady at the end of the street named Martha Gower. She sometimes rents out a

117

room to travelers. There's a sign with her name on it in front of the house.'

'I thank you, brother,' Hobie said. 'I'm a little weary and my pony is plain wore down.'

Hobie wavered; it was risky. But he might have no better time to ask someone. 'Any of you men know where a man named Casey might be living these days?'

'Which Casey?' the man who appeared to be intoxicated asked belligerently.

'I don't know. I once came across the trail of a man named Casey who said he lived up around here somewhere.' Hobie tried to be nonchalant in his answer, but it was obvious that there had been some damage done. The men withdrew into their tight group and ignored him.

'Thank you,' Hobie said and heeled his pony forward at a walk. Whoever Casey was, it seemed he was not loved by everyone. In a way, he reflected, that was good. No one would be inclined to ride out to the farm and tell Casey that someone had arrived in town asking questions about him.

Maybe.

At the end of the street where it dipped into darkness again, Casey came upon a little brown house with a white picket fence around its front yard and a hand-painted sign that read, 'Gower'.

Slipping from the saddle, Hobie took a minute to stretch the miles from his back and legs and then

118

went in the wooden gate. There was a small brass bell affixed to the gate, which tinkled as he entered.

'State your name and your business,' a voice called from the front porch of the darkened house. Dark, it was, but not so dark that Hobie could not see that the challenge was backed by a shotgun leveled in his direction.

EIGHT

Hobie raised his hands without having been commanded to, and he replied in the meekest voice he could manage, 'My name's Hobie Lee, and I'm only a poor traveling man.'

'Come ahead and let me take a look at you,' the voice answered.

The shotgun never wavered as Hobie approached the woman in the brown dress who stood on the porch as if guarding the place. Her hair was gray, arranged in a scraggly bun. Her face was bovine except that there was more anger on it than you are likely to see on a cow. Sixty years old, at a guess, she wore the unhappiness of many unfulfilled years as an expression.

'You don't look too dangerous,' she said. 'What are you doing here, young man?'

'Well, if you are Martha Gower, I was told in town that you sometimes let travelers have a bed in your house for a consideration.'

'You have a "consideration" on you, do you?'

'Yes, ma'am, I do,' Hobie replied. He did in fact have a few dollars which he had found in the sack of provisions Trish had left for him. A last, generous gift, rightly suspecting that Hobie would have a need for funds somewhere in his travels.

'Well, come on in the house. I want to have a better look at you and see the shine of your consideration. And I want you to tell me again who you are and what trail you could have wandered from to find your way to this godforsaken little village.'

The house was not small, but of a comfortable size. The kitchen was roomy and warm, the table had a white cloth covering it. Hobie was invited, and sat down, his hat on his lap. He was offered tea and accepted it. He had no liking for the stuff, but considered it polite to take it. Served in a teacup with flowers painted on it, Hobie tasted it, nodded and then mostly stared at the liquid. He was wondering where to start asking about the mysterious Casey. It would probably be best to start some conversation first; after all, Mrs Gower could be an aunt, a close friend, a distant relative. It wouldn't do to make accusations, especially since all of his knowledge was second-hand.

'Have you lived here for quite some time?' Hobie asked.

'Forever. Came here forty years ago when

someone found a pocket of gold in the hills. It didn't last long. It was played out within five years, and my husband was gone by then.'

'He died?'

Martha Gower smiled; an old smile. 'No, he's only dead to me. Of course, by now, who knows? Henry Gower made the acquaintance of liquor and a saloon girl – I don't know which came first. Later I heard the girl left him, so he was rid of her. He never could get rid of his liking for hard liquor. That was forty years ago, Hobie Lee. I should have left, I know. Now,' she shrugged, 'I've no place to go, and I realize that life holds nothing more for me. So I stay.'

'I see,' Hobie said. It was time, so he asked, 'Have you ever heard of a man called Casey? He's supposed to have a farm in this area.'

'Bill Casey?' Her face twisted into a sour expression. 'What do you want with him, since you're just traveling through? You aren't some sort of lawman, are you?' she asked. Her hands, Hobie noticed, were clenched tightly around her teacup. Her brown eyes were focused sternly on Hobie's.

'No, I'm not.'

'Too bad. Bill Casey belongs in prison. No, he deserves to hang. The men in my husband's day would have done that.'

'I don't know anything about the man,' Hobie said. 'But I had heard the name somewhere, and I was looking for a place to stay.'

'That would be a fine place – if you wanted your throat cut in your sleep,' the old lady said, not making an attempt to hide her antipathy.

'He, uh . . .' Hobie tried to choose his words carefully, 'is considered a bad man around here?'

Martha rose abruptly; standing over him, she said with uncontrolled anger, 'Bill Casey is considered a bad man in whatever place he finds himself. I see you've had enough tea, and I believe I've had enough conversation, Hobie Lee. Show me the coin you said you had, and I'll show you a place where you can sleep.'

The woman didn't trust him; that was obvious. He had said too much, but how else was he to find Casey, and the farm where Ceci Starr was supposedly being held captive?

The room Hobie was shown to was small, smelling of disuse. Hobie doubted that Mrs Gower had paying guests often. He knew that she was eager enough to accept payment in advance. He closed the door, undressed and went to bed, thinking as he lay there, studying the ceiling, that he would not be so fortunate as to have a bed on this night were it not for the generosity of Trish Fisher.

Morning, seen through the single window of the small room, was bright and clear. The weather was not threatening. In the old woman's back yard, the young trees were in bud. A handful of smaller birds hopped around the ground, peeping bird messages

123

to one another.

Before turning in, Hobie had placed his paint pony in a small horse shed and the paint was nibbling at alfalfa hay which Hobie had also purchased. The animal, as usual, was ready to hit the trail.

Hobie saddled his horse and led it back to the front of the house. Martha Gower, wearing the same brown dress, stood on the porch, arms crossed. Her expression was not disapproving; neither was it cheerful.

'I see you're checking out,' she said, coming down the steps toward Hobie.

'Yes, ma'am. I've got to be going on my way.'

She shook her head. 'I've got to believe that you're still determined to find Bill Casey – I won't try to guess the reason. If you were to continue on down the road,' she said, pointing, 'you'll find a fork in the road where three oak trees stand together. If you follow the trail to your left, you'll reach the farm about a half a mile on.'

She added before turning away, 'And if you take the road to your right, you'll be traveling away from grief.'

'Thank you for your concern,' Hobie said, stepping into his stirrup, 'but you see, I've sort of got an obligation to fulfill.'

'All right, then,' Martha Gower said as Hobie settled into his saddle. 'I can only wish you luck.' She hesitated. 'You didn't eat no breakfast, and that's included in my price. Take this,' she said, handing Hobie a small sack. 'I hard-boiled you a couple of eggs and made a bacon sandwich you can eat along the trail.'

There was an unexpected softness in the woman's eyes that Hobie could not understand. He only muttered his thanks, turned the paint's head and rode past the open gate. When he looked back, Martha Gower was closing the gate, her face weathered and old once again.

He came upon the three live-oak trees standing beside the fork in the road before he had finished his sack-breakfast and sat his horse, chewing. Left or right? There was really no choice, but then again the last time he had come upon a fork in the road he had made the wrong decision. He guided the horse on to the trail toward the farm, having no idea of what he would find there except that it was dangerous ground.

Maybe Gene Brady had gotten it all wrong. Perhaps Cecilia Starr was content where she was, waiting for Hal Bassett to arrive. Maybe Gene had been given a chance to leave, would not and was given a rough farewell at Ceci's suggestion. Who knew?

He might be able to find out how things stood if he could talk to Ceci alone, but the odds of that occurring were very long. He realized that if that happened, his impulse would be just to snatch her

125

and ride like fury with Ceci screaming and kicking. There didn't seem to be a good answer to his problem. Pretend he was a friend of Bassett? He would be unmasked with a few minutes of conversation. Try to get the drop on four armed, watchful men? Ridiculous in the extreme. So what was there to do?

And what exactly are you doing here at all, Hobie Lee?

He could have stayed back at the Wonder Mine with Trish, doing some light work she had promised him, and lived pleasantly through the spring and summer with nothing more to worry about than avoiding Boomer's insistent fists. Instead he had chosen to go tilting at windmills.

Hobie had called himself a fool in the past, but even a fool would have more sense than to walk into a situation like this one. No, he was beyond foolish; he was crazy. The White Wind had blown away all of his common sense. He was under the spell of madness.

With his head up, but his eyes barely focused, he rode on, nearly passing the man who sat his buckskin horse at the side of the road. A familiar voice called out to him.

'Hobie! Hobie Lee?'

Hobie blinked, spun his head as his hand dropped toward his holstered revolver. The man on the buckskin laughed.

'Don't shoot,' Calvin Winslow said, and the SD

foreman started his horse toward Hobie, smiling as he came.

Cal Winslow looked rested, shaved and seemed to be in a good humor. 'What in the world are you dong way out here, Hobie?'

'Seeing the sights,' Hobie said lightly, but he saw there was no sense in kidding Cal – the man knew.

'How about you?' Hobie asked. 'What in the world brings you up here, Cal? And how did you know this was where she was?'

'Let's pull off the road,' Calvin Winslow suggested, looking ahead. They rode into a cottonwood grove a little way from the trail. Winslow swung down from his buckskin and Hobie followed suit.

'Have you seen her yet?' Winslow asked without preamble.

'I just got here. What about you, Cal? And how did you find out anything about this situation?'

'From Hal Bassett, of course,' Winslow said, and Hobie could only stare at the man.

'You talked to Hal Bassett?' Hobie asked in disbelief.

'You could put it that way,' Cal answered drily. 'I had that opportunity after he had his ransom demand delivered to the Starr-Diamond.'

'Ransom. . . ? Is that why he snatched her?'

'So it seems.'

'But Ceci, I imagine, thought she was running off to live with her lover.'

127

'So she did, I would guess. That's what Hal Bassett had in mind, too, but he wanted some sort of dowry. Gabe Starr would never have allowed Bassett on the SD, let alone will the ranch to Ceci if Bassett was going to take over after the old man died.'

'I see,' Hobie said.

'Bassett was damned if he was going to give it up with nothing in his pockets. A few days ago he sent a messenger in with a ransom note. The messenger didn't have a lot of heart; after I had a talk with him he led me back to where Bassett was waiting for his reply.'

'And he talked to you?'

'He talked,' Winslow said. His eyes were very cold now. 'I didn't give him an option.'

'I see,' Hobie said in a lower voice. 'After you talked to him, did you have him arrested?'

'That didn't seem like a good idea. He would have gotten out again some time.'

Hobie asked no more questions about Bassett's fate. Winslow's answer was clear. 'So what were you going to do now?' he asked.

'Get Ceci home,' Winslow said firmly. 'How, I'm not exactly sure.'

'That's what I came to do as well. To clear my name and get her home to her father. I'm not sure how to go about it myself, though.'

'Well,' Winslow said, looking in the direction of the farm, 'at least we've managed to double our force, Hobie. Maybe we can come up with something between us.'

The two sat and talked for a time. There was no good plan they could come up with, but Calvin Winslow suggested that one of them ride to the far side of the farm, taking a circuitous route. That man – Winslow decided that it should be Hobie without any discussion of the matter – was to start a ruckus there, firing his guns to draw the kidnappers, at least some of them, in that direction. Then the other – Cal Winslow – would be able to approach from this side without having to worry about more than a couple of men. He could either invent some kind of story to keep them off, or go to shooting. Whichever option was presented to him.

Hobie didn't like it; he liked none of it, but he had no better idea. Stealth would not work, and they were going to have to start shooting one way or the other.

'The more rounds you can get off, the better,' Winslow advised. 'Use your rifle and handgun both. They won't know what's up. They might think that Bassett has returned followed by a posse. It doesn't matter what they think,' he added grimly, 'we're taking Ceci before the sun goes down. Or we'll both be planted in a cornfield.'

Not a cheery thought, but Hobie had known it would come to this. No matter that he hadn't let his mind dwell on it, there was no way these hardened men were going to let the girl go without a battle.

Winslow asked, 'What do you know of these men, Hobie, if anything?'

Hobie told him what Gene Brady had learned about them, but, after listening, Winslow could only shrug. 'The names mean nothing to me. Probably they were just home-grown toughs or a part of the Bassett gang. No matter, I don't care what their handles are.' Winslow rose, his face confident, set. Hobie wondered at the older man's composure, but then maybe after killing Hal Bassett, Winslow felt that he was fated to win the war.

Winslow did not feel the gusting White Wind.

As for Hobie, riding in a wide arc toward the far side of the farm, he felt real concern, if not actual dread. He had no wish to end up feeding next year's corn crop.

The day was still. There were the sounds of squawking crows, the startled rush of a deer escaping into the forest, but no man-sounds, no dogs barking. No farmers worked the soil and no sentries on horseback appeared. But the gang members could be concealed in any clump of low-growing trees, behind the gray, mossy boulders which studded the land.

Hobie came upon a narrow, lazily running silver creek, and figured he had come far enough for his purpose, which was to be a decoy for Winslow as he rushed the house and tried to rescue Ceci Starr. Hobie figured that he had probably drawn the easier job, but he would have liked to be there when Ceci felt saved. Cal Winslow would take the glory for that, and he probably would deserve it. And Ceci would be more likely to trust the SD foreman, more encouraged to ride with him than she would with Hobie Lee. Hobie mentally slapped himself – it was no time to be thinking about glory.

Hobie debated leaving his horse picketed away from him, with the racket he was going to cause, but decided he would rather keep the paint pony near at hand in case he was forced to make a sudden retreat.

He had bellied down into the long grass along the creek when he saw the sun glint off something bright, worn or carried by the figure of a man, distant yet menacing. Had he been spotted? It could be a part of their regular patrol to circle the house and fields, but this shadowy figure seemed to be walking directly toward him.

The man was too far off for even a decent rifle shot; though Hobie's job was to raise a ruckus on this side of the farm and draw attention to himself, it was too early to start the game. He had no idea if Calvin Winslow was set or not – one more flaw in a plan riddled with them. Still Hobie hesitated, not wanting to frighten the man into rushing back to the house with a warning.

He had the man in the iron sights of his Winchester, but did not want to fire. He did not wish to kill the man, nor was it wise to miss the attempt.

Sweat had trickled down from his forehead and was stinging his eyes. Hobie glanced back to make sure his paint pony was still where he had left it. It was a good thing that he did, for, beyond the horse, Hobie saw the shadow of a man approaching his position on foot. He moved in a crouched run, carrying a rifle in both hands. Well, damnit all! Hobie had never really wanted to kill any of the bad men even though he knew it was the only way out of here. He forced himself to quit thinking of the tracking men as human beings. They were only animals intent on killing him.

It was a rough shot he took, but well calculated. He saw his stalker dart behind a screen of brush, and Hobie was ready for him when he exited at a loping run. Leading the figure with his front bead sight, Hobie squeezed off a round from the .44-.40 rifle.

The man crumpled up and threw his rifle away. His eyes were wide, his mouth was open in a soundless scream. His hat had flown free and Hobie saw that he was nearly as bald as an egg. He was also very heavy, his body nearly round. Hobie figured he had just killed the man called Turk. He hated the idea – he had just taken the life of a man he had never known.

He had to remind himself that these were members of a kidnapping gang, that they had beaten Gene Brady half to death, and were probably capable of harming Ceci if they did not get what they wanted.

Hobie shrugged off all of these deeper thoughts in half a second when he turned his eyes back to look for the man who had been approaching him from the farmhouse.

He was gone!

Hobie lay on his stomach, searching the sun-bright fields for the man, but he had simply disappeared from the land. Remembering the original plan, Hobie fired his rifle twice into the air and then drew his Colt and loosed another two rounds. It might sound as if two men were involved in a gun-fight. Maybe Turk's friend would try to work his way forward to help out.

'How goes the war?' a voice from behind Hobie said.

Hobie moved as quickly as he had in his life, rolling on to his back. He had both the Winchester and his pistol in his hands, and he fired them simultaneously, wildly, as the man with the black handlebar mustache sighted his own pistol. Three close explosions sounded nearly together. The bullet fired at Hobie missed his head by bare inches, spraying him with the sand of the river-bed.

Hobie had let the rifle fall free and was thumbing back the hammer of his Colt desperately. The man with the mustache – the one Gene Brady had called Arnie – was on his feet, the hammer of his own Colt ratcheted back.

Arnie did not fire again. He couldn't.

There was blood fountaining from a chest wound, washing over his blue shirt and leather vest. His eyes were wide and white, somehow expressionless. He nodded once to Hobie and toppled forward to bury his face in the sand.

Arnie did not rise, would not rise again. Hobie Lee felt the twitching beginning in his own legs work its way upward. His hands began to tremble, his teeth were chattering. Well, Hobie thought, no one ever named me for a hero. He was just plain sick and angry with himself, even though if he faced it rationally, the two kidnappers had given him no choice: kill or be killed.

Hobie didn't like either option, but he supposed his was the best. He lived.

The paint pony, which had patiently stayed in place initially, had now broken its tether and was gone. The close shooting had been just too much for the horse to bear. Hobie tried to whistle it up and then went tramping through the brush, looking for it. He found the paint, drinking from the creek. Its eyes were wary; it tossed its mottled head in accusation.

'I know,' Hobie said to it in a calm voice. 'That wasn't much fun, was it?'

He was swinging into leather again when a flurry of gunshots in the direction of the farmhouse filled the air. Hobie heeled his pony forward. What now? Apparently Cal Winslow had reached the house. Cal was still alive or the peaceful day wouldn't be rife with gunfire. Hobie wrestled with indecision.

He could not just go charging across the open ground surrounding the house. He would be too clear a target for the kidnappers. Yet if he did not ride to assist Calvin, the whole rescue attempt would be wasted effort. And Ceci would still be in the hands of the rough men.

Riding low across the withers of his horse, Hobie raced toward the house, flagging the pony with the ends of his reins. The shots continued, although he could not judge the shooters' positions. At least, he thought, they're not shooting at me.

Someone emerged stealthily from the back door of the house, rifle in his hands. The man did not glance Hobie's way as he began to circle the building; apparently they had devised some strategy to catch Cal Winslow off guard.

Hobie hurried the horse a little more. Now it seemed to be running in slow motion, but they were covering ground rapidly. As the kidnapper disappeared around a corner of the house, Hobie debated fractionally whether to remain mounted or to swing down and fight on foot. On foot, he had decided, for it meant a surer shot, when another figure appeared in the open back doorway of the house.

Ceci Starr. She saw Hobie, waved her hands frantically and then threw them skyward. He slowed the hard-ridden paint and approached Ceci, Colt in hand. 'What's happening?' Hobie wanted to know.

'Bill Casey is at the front window; he sent the Texan to circle behind Calvin – that is Calvin, isn't it?

'It's Calvin,' Hobie answered. The girl with the porcelain-doll face had tears welling up in her blue eyes. Her hair, Hobie noticed, was neatly brushed and pinned up, not a loose strand falling free. Cecilia Starr was clutching at his leg, her eyes pathetic.

'You're here. Hobie Lee, take me out of this. I heard about the reward offered. Get me back to the SD and I'll see that it's yours.' Wearing a long black skirt, she seemed determined to mount the paint behind Hobie.

'What about Calvin?' Hobie asked, His blood was running cold. Possibly because he had never had the girl kiss him on the mouth.

'He knows what he's doing.'

'I don't. I don't even know what you're up to,' Hobie said. 'Make a dash toward the forest. I'm not running out on Cal now.'

Her eyes hesitated, found fury and scraped against his scornfully. Then she hoisted her skirt and took off at a decent running pace toward the verge of the concealing pine forest. Hobie had only two choices. He had let the Texan outdistance him as he stopped to talk to Ceci. The other choice was not one he pre-ferred – walk into that farmhouse and try bracing Bill Casey.

Hobie slipped from the saddle and, as silently as he could, approached the back door of the house while in front of it guns blazed away, shattering the peace of the morning. Hobie, pistol in hand, stepped on to the porch and entered the back door of the house.

NINE

The report of a pistol fired close at hand reverberated through the small house. Acrid gunsmoke crawled along the low ceiling. Hobie peered into the front room from the kitchen, Colt in his hand, his body shielded by the wall. Kneeling beside the front window was the man named Bill Casey. When Hobie saw him, he was hastily thumbing fresh cartridges into the cylinder of his revolver.

Now was as good a time as any, Hobie decided. With only his right arm and gun hand visible to anyone in the other room, Hobie said in a controlled voice, 'Drop your weapon, Casey. No need to die.'

'Who—?' Bill Casey turned his eyes from the window, growled a low curse and fired three wild shots in Hobie's direction. Lead whined off kitchen utensils and broke the back kitchen window. Hobie had been holding his aim, and now, with no other choice, he fired back.

On his knees still, Casey clutched his stomach, then sprawled forward to kiss the hardwood floor.

Hobie gave him a minute, but there was no sign of life in Casey's body. Not a finger twitched. Hobie Lee moved to the front window cautiously. Outside the gun battle continued. There was a storm of gunfire and then a sporadic few reports. Finally there was one last gunshot which seemed somehow definitive, then silence.

Hobie Lee went to the door and opened it a bare crack. The two men out there had finished their violent discussion and Hobie needed to know what the outcome had been. It was a little chancy, but Hobie had to take the risk.

'Calvin!' he yelled across the field. Someone was moving among the pine trees across the road.

'Hobie Lee!' Calvin's cry came back. 'Is everything all right over there?'

'It's safe – come on in!'

Holstering his gun Hobie turned away from the door, leaving it ajar. There was a gusting breeze outside and it swept through the house, whipping away the gunsmoke. Hobie looked down at Bill Casey, not liking the sight. He had not gotten in this to kill, but to try to save a girl's life. Apparently everyone disliked the bad man; that didn't mean he needed killing – not to Hobie anyway.

He would never make an executioner.

Calvin Winslow's boots scraped across the porch

beyond, and the door was flung open. Cal's pistol was in his hand. The foreman's eyes went to the body crumpled on the floor and then to Hobie's.

'Good work, cowboy,' Calvin said, holstering his sidearm. 'There's no more of them around?'

'There were only four of them that I know of; all four are dead.'

Calvin nodded with satisfaction, took a deep breath and tucked in his shirt. 'All right, where is Ceci?'

'I sent her off to hide in the woods,' Hobie said.

'That was a good idea. Let's gather up one of the spare horses and go looking for her.'

They didn't have to look for long. Cecilia Starr emerged from the pine woods as soon as she saw them. She was waving hysterically as she ran toward them. Calvin was out of his saddle before she reached them and the two fell together in a lengthy embrace. Hobie frowned, staying back, holding the extra horse they had collected for Ceci on a tether. The two lovers exchanged rapid, garbled words not meant for Hobie's ears.

Finally they walked back and Hobie handed the lead to the red roan Ceci had been using to Calvin. She swung into leather smoothly, not needing Calvin Winslow's offered assistance. The wind was becoming blustery and a few low clouds drifted in their direction from the high mountains beyond, like wisps of smoke being blown from dead candles. The air felt heavier, cooler. Hobie was thinking that they might be in for a rainstorm.

'Which way now?' Hobie asked.

'Which way? Why, right back to the SD, Hobie Lee,' Cal answered.

'What I meant was, I didn't think you'd want to follow the road back out. There could be more of the gang that we don't know about.'

'That's true,' Calvin said thoughtfully as his eyes moved around the fields and forested hills. 'Tell you what, let's take to the timber and parallel the road as best we can. I just want to put some distance between us and this place.'

So they proceeded, riding through the pine woods as the rising wind rattled the boughs of the big trees. Now and then a gust would shake pine cones free of their branches and small dead wood would fall. Hobie noticed that there were no squirrels about and they were not followed by mocking blue jays. The wild things knew that a storm was coming.

Riding wide of Lassen, they rode a straight line, or as close to one as they could manage in the hill country, toward the distant Starr-Diamond Ranch. Hobie's paint pony was exhausted as they crested yet another in a long stretch of low hills. The sky was coloring, and to the north it was the color of smoky embers. The first raindrops began to fall as they once again entered deep timber.

141

'I think we should hold up,' Hobie said, 'my pony is beat.'

Cal Winslow glanced at Hobie, then at the sky, which was roofed over with cold clouds. Rain was filtering through the forest. 'You're right, Hobie Lee. Keep your eyes open for something that offers a little shelter.'

'What about that?' Hobie said, gesturing toward his right at a sheer standing wall of granite. 'It'll cut the wind and we can see if there isn't some hollow to hole up in. We won't be able to see to ride much longer.'

'Let's take a look,' Calvin agreed, turning his horse in the direction of the rock, face which rose 200 feet or more. The wind had become punishing. It was a relief just to reach the stone bulwark where its force was cut. In the near-darkness they began searching for some sort of shelter. They rode along the base of the massive bluff for a quarter of a mile in the driving rain before Hobie held up his hand and gestured into the darkness. By a flash of lightning he had caught a glimpse of what proved to be a hollow eroded into the cliff face. It was no more than ten feet deep and about fifty feet long. Poor enough shelter, but it was a place to weather out the night. As they proceeded that way a bolt of lightning struck a nearby towering twin pine and the tree blazed with fire, fizzled in the rain and stood swaying, scorched and black in the silver rain. As thunder rumbled,

Hobie trembled. If that had been a few feet closer. . . .

They dismounted and crowded into the hollow. The horses did not like the place for some reason, perhaps its closeness, and so Hobie took the three of them to a nearby fallen tree and tethered them there. They would have to suffer until the storm had blown past. 'Your own fault,' he said to his mournful paint. 'There was room enough for you.'

Maybe the other horses had given it bad advice.

Hobie trudged back to the hollow. Calvin Winslow had managed to start a small fire from dry wood found in the shelter. It wasn't much for warmth, but its brightness seemed to make the stormy night more bearable.

A dozen steps from the fire Hobie became aware of some shuffling creature following along. He started to turn, but a human voice growled, 'You just put your hands up and keep them there. You're not in this – so stay out of it, get me?'

Hobie nodded silently and raised his hands. The voice was raspy, as if the man's throat were filled with stones – or blood? He managed to glance back and saw that the shaggy beast following him walked with a hobbling drunken gait. He was half-bent over as if his stomach pained him terribly.

'Who are—?' Hobie tried to ask, but the man reminded him:

'I told you you're not in this – stay out of it!'

143

Hobie approached the fire. Cal Winslow looked up and so did Ceci, who had been warming her hands there. It was Ceci who cried out.

'Hal! He told me that you were dead! Otherwise I would never have—'

'Shut up, Ceci!' Hal Bassett replied savagely. 'You know damn well that you'd have done whatever you needed to do to win. You, Winslow,' Bassett said as he switched the sights of his pistol toward the SD foreman. 'Cowardly bastard! To gut-shoot me and then take off with the money and go after my woman!'

'Hal!' Ceci pleaded, her face anguished, hands clenched. But it was too late, because Calvin Winslow had already gone for his gun. Hal Bassett had the drop, and he was quicker in firing. Cal took lead, took it hard, high on his chest, and he spun around, pitching forward toward the fire. Ceci's face was a mask of horror.

Bassett took three staggering steps forward. His hair hung in his face. There was mud on his shirt, on his jeans.

'Don't shoot me, Hal!' Ceci cried. 'I was meaning to—'

Bassett interrupted her. 'I don't care what you were meaning to do,' he said in short, gasping words. 'But I won't kill you. I'll leave you to live out the rest of your life in your privately constructed hell. How could anything so perfect in form be so. . . ?'

Bassett said no more. He seated himself on the ground, cross-legged. Then, after a minute, he toppled over to die next to the man he had killed. Ceci was shaking; her lips moved wordlessly, but after a few minutes of violent trembling she pulled herself together. She looked at Hobie and said, 'It wasn't supposed to end this way.' Then, as if shrugging all of the violence and mayhem aside, she said, 'Well, at least I've still got you and the saddle-bags full of money. I made sure that Cal still had the ransom.'

Hobie Lee looked down at the two dead men, the firelight flickering over their still forms. Which of the two had been more guilty? As Hobie now understood it, Hal Bassett had plotted to have his own lover kidnapped and ask her father for a ransom. Calvin Winslow had volunteered to deliver it for Gabe Starr. Cal had roughed up the messenger, found out where Bassett was waiting and proceeded there to gun Bassett down, while Ceci waited at the farmhouse. She must have been angry when Bassett didn't show up as planned, but when Cal arrived and she realized that he had the ransom and was equally smitten with her and the opportunity to take over the SD, she easily changed course.

She was that kind of woman.

'I'll see you home,' Hobie said in a flat voice. 'Because that's what I set out to do. I don't care about the money. Take it back and tell Gabe any tale that you can dream up. Your father won't want to see me, and I don't want to see him. He'll still hold me responsible for your disappearance, and who knows what story you'll tell him to get me in deeper trouble.

'I'm taking you home, but that's it, Ceci. You've never kissed my mouth.'

God save all the men she had kissed.

The storm had passed and the morning was bright and clear when they reached the hilltop overlooking the sprawling Starr-Diamond Ranch. The men below were working the cattle; another gather was in progress. How many friends Hobie would never see again were down there, joking, laughing, enjoying the spring morning? Men the White Wind had not touched.

Cecilia Starr turned her fairy-book blue eyes toward Hobie and offered, 'Come on to the house with me. I'm sure I can straighten everything out.'

'I'm sure you can,' Hobie said. 'But I don't want to be present to hear it.' He shook his head. 'Go on home, Ceci. I haven't got a word more to say to you.'

She started to speak again. Her mouth opened but closed again without uttering a sound. He watched as the woman trailed down toward Gabe Starr's house, undoubtedly to a warm welcome. What tale she would spin, Hobie could not guess, but he was certain that her powers of invention were up to it. She could explain away the kidnapping, the death of Cal Winslow, the absence of Hobie Lee and Gene Brady, how she had come to retrieve the ransom money in her saddle-bags, what had happened to Hal Bassett.

Yes, she could. She was a woman quite remarkable in her way.

Hobie turned his horse toward the distant town of Osborne. There was nothing there, but there was even less for him remaining on the SD.

Sundown found Hobie walking his paint along Osborne's main street, his eyes searching the buildings, the passers-by idly. A once-familiar voice called out as he passed a green-painted saloon.

'Hobie Lee!'

Hobie halted his horse and turned his head. In front of the saloon stood a man in a white apron holding a broom. Hobie squinted in that direction, the dimness making identification difficult. The man waved a hand.

'Gene!' Hobie said, starting his paint that way. 'How in the world are you?'

'Ah, I'm doing all right, Hobie,' the young man from Kansas said. 'Right now I've got me a job swamping out the saloon. Me and old Randy Dalton got us a room at the hotel. He was walking around pretty well this morning. So he'll be able to find some kind of work soon, too. What about you, Hobie?'

That was a fair question for which Hobie had no answer.

How was he doing? Well, he was alive. He gave Gene the usual sort of answer to that question, wished him luck and started on his way.

In the morning, after a comfortable night in the hotel, he went to breakfast and considered that he was still living on Trish's generosity. The money was nearly gone, but there was still time to thank her. He decided to ride out to the Wonder Mine. He was ready to take on any sort of work Trish could find for him up there. He doubted he would be any good at mucking out saloons.

The road was still familiar; the sign still stood at the fork. He guided his pony toward the road that led up to the Wonder. There didn't seem to be as much activity at the mine as during his last visit. Maybe most of it was going on underground. Riding his horse slowly into the yard he started toward the mine office.

A narrow man he had never seen before held up a hand and shouted, 'Hey you! Where do you think you're going?'

'To the office,' Hobie answered.

The thin man had approached and put a hand on the paint pony's bridle, which Hobie didn't like.

'Not with those guns on you, you're not,' the stranger said. 'We got a rule out here – no weapons, and that especially means in the office.'

'Sorry,' Hobie Lee muttered. 'I'd forgotten.'

'Just unbuckle that Colt,' the man said, and then,

without asking, he slipped Hobie's Winchester from its sheath. 'I'll put these in that storage shed over there.' He nodded toward a small outbuilding to the side of the office.

Hobie didn't intend to get into an argument, so he did as he was instructed, handing his gunbelt to the mine worker.

'What was it you were wanting exactly?' the thin man asked. 'We ain't hiring, if that was it.'

'No? Well, I was wanting to see Miss Patricia Fisher, if she's available.'

'She's not available around here,' the man said with a shake of his head. 'Mizz Fisher. She took off a few days ago – on her way to Wyoming.'

Trish? Gone? She had indicated that she intended to work here for a while, that she wasn't planning on going back to her uncle's house in Laramie. Hobie frowned.

'Are you sure?' he asked.

'I know whether somebody's here or gone,' replied the narrow man.

'Maybe I'd better talk to Mr Schaeffer or Mr Suggs then.'

'Suit yourself,' the stranger said. 'Though they'll tell you the same thing.' Then he tramped off with Hobie's guns. One of those men who is pleased with himself for wielding the smallest bit of power.

Still puzzled, Hobie continued toward the mine office. He swung down from his horse and spent a minute stretching out the saddle kinks.

'Lose another lap, pup?' a familiar, ugly voice asked. 'It must be hard trying to keep track of all of your women.'

Hobie turned around slowly. Boomer was not more than three paces from him. His face was red and set with anger, his meaty fists clenched.

'I didn't come here to fight with you,' Hobie said.

'Well, lapdog, that isn't your choice.'

'Look, Boomer, I don't know what it is you don't like about me, but—'

'I can't stand a man who makes his way living off women while I'm down in a hole in the ground waiting for the roof to cave in at any moment, waiting to see if I can set one more charge without blowing myself up!' Boomer's voice rose in volume as he went on. 'Then I remember some little puppy up above the ground who's sitting on some lady's lap nibbling bonbons from her little white hand.

'I work like a dog and the puppy gets the candy. It ain't fair!'

'You've got things all wrong, Boomer. It seems like you made up your mind who I was first and then started looking for reasons you thought that. I would never have come to the Wonder at all if I hadn't been shot along the road.'

'Yeah,' Boomer said, moving closer, 'I should kick myself for that; when you went down I was sure I'd finished you.'

'*You!* You're the one who shot me, Boomer? A cowardly ambush? I thought you were more of a man than that.'

'I was just tired of playing with you,' Boomer said, moving ever closer so that now Hobie could smell the rank odor of accumulated sweat on the big man. 'I decided to finish the matter the easy way.' Boomer smiled, or at least the grimace on his fleshy mouth could have been interpreted as a smile. 'As to how much of a man I am, I thought I already taught you that. I'd be happy to demonstrate again.'

'It took three of you last time, if I recall,' Hobie said. 'Should I wait while you call your gang?'

That gibe infuriated Boomer. His whole bulky body could be seen to tense, and the smile, or whatever the expression had been, narrowed to a tight line. His eyes widened. His fists bunched into ham-sized clubs.

'We don't need to wait for anything,' Boomer said. 'I'm going to beat you to death.'

Boomer plodded in, a bear of a man with coal dust clinging to his overalls, mud on his boots and pure fury on his wide face. Hobie backed away, felt his back come up against his horse and stepped away, trying to get more space to work in. He was not going to outslug the miner, but he might be able to elude some of the punishing blows, perhaps long enough for the mine bosses to stop the fight. Trish had told him that brawling was not allowed on the Wonder either, but it seemed that no one knew about the fight or was inclined to try to halt it.

Boomer cocked his right arm and threw a tremendous punch overhand which Hobie managed to slip away from enough so it bounced painfully but harmlessly off his shoulder. Hobie, both hands in front of his face, jabbed a straight left into Boomer's fleshy face. Boomer only smiled. Hobie jabbed again, circling to his left. This shot landed squarely on Boomer's nose. The big man didn't like it but he grunted a laugh. When Hobie threw a third jab at Boomer's face, he drew blood from the big man's nose. Boomer quit laughing and hunched his shoulders, moving in with grim determination.

Hobie jabbed again and tried a right cross which bounced harmlessly off Boomer's jaw just below his ear. Hobie decided that he could pretty much hit Boomer at will. The big man had no defense, but he had never bothered to learn any. His way of fighting was simply to wade in and maul his opponent. He could hit Boomer, but the miner seemed not to even feel the effect of Hobie Lee's best shots.

Hobie's boot slipped on a small rock underfoot, and to regain his balance, he unfortunately stepped forward and into the crushing blow of one of Boomer's right hand blows. The miner's fist slammed into Hobie's ribs and if Boomer hadn't broken a few of them, he had definitely bruised them badly. Hobie stepped away, gasping for breath. As he did Boomer charged with a barrage of blows, left and right, which sent Hobie to his knees.

Rising again as Boomer watched, panting and smirking, taunting Hobie, Hobie saw that a crowd of miners had gathered for the entertainment. On the porch of the mine office, Schaeffer and Suggs in their gray suits also stood watching the proceedings. It was obvious that no one was going to try to stop this fight.

Hobie found himself growing angry. He made the decision to have done with it quickly. Let Boomer have his victory, but Hobie was going to put some pain on the big man in the meantime if he could. No more dancing away, trying to fend off Boomer's wild blows.

'Let's have at it,' Hobie said in a dangerously low voice, and Boomer blinked at the cowboy.

Hobie already knew that Boomer's strategy ignored defense, and so he decided to take it to the miner by throwing as many punches as he could, not singly, but in rapid combinations. All of these might be negated by a single trip-hammer blow from Boomer, but anyway, it would be ended. He did not think the mine bosses would go so far as to allow Boomer to stomp Hobie to death once he was down.

With wild energy Hobie threw himself at Boomer. A right and a left both got through to bang against opposite temples and before Boomer could fire a shot back, Hobie, working with fury and superior speed, managed an uppercut which snapped Boomer's teeth together. Before Boomer had recovered from that, Hobie landed a right to Boomer's eye and a left to his ear. Boomer hit him with a mighty blow to his jaw, and Hobie saw colored stars behind his eyes, but there was no pain. Not in the middle of this.

Moving close in against Boomer's chest to shield himself from the big man's power, Hobie threw another uppercut. He heard a grunt from Boomer. Boomer had bitten off the tip of his own tongue. Blood now flowed from Boomer's mouth, leaked from his ear. Hobie could see that the miner's left eye was slowly closing behind a bruised swelling.

Someone in the gathered crowd yelled out something. Whether it was encouragement for Boomer or for himself, Hobie could not tell. The outer world seemed to have vanished into a dense fog. There was only the steady, rapid unleashing of his own savage blows and the occasional crushing force of one of Boomer's terrific shots.

Boomer's fists landed with great force, and they jarred Hobie each time they struck, but the big man's fighting style left him to take three, four or five shots for every one he delivered. Hobie felt Boomer back away from him a step and a malicious glee came over him as he rained blows, straight, overhand, upward on the miner's head and face.

Now Boomer did try to cover up, holding both of

154

his fists in front of his bloody face, but one of Hobie's right crosses sneaked through the miner's defense and Boomer's eyes went blank. Seeing this Hobie only increased his assault. He realized that he was hitting an unconscious man as Boomer's arms lowered to his side, but he did not stop until he felt hands on his shoulder, pulling him away, Men had also caught hold of Boomer, and their bodies were the only thing holding him on his feet. The big man swayed, stumbled and sagged in the arms of his fellow miners.

Several men offered congratulation to Hobie but he shrugged off their pointless acclaim and staggered toward the mine office. His ears were ringing, his legs were unsteady, his ribs felt crushed and mangled.

'They tell me Trish is gone,' Hobie said, holding his battered ribs with one hand, looking up at the mine bosses through a screen of his own hair.

'I thought you knew that,' the portly Tyrone Schaeffer answered.

'She's gone,' the sharp-faced, sharp-tongued Walter Suggs spat. 'I suggest you do the same.'

With that the mine bosses stepped from the porch and walked away. Hobie heard Suggs mutter, 'And now our only powder man might be laid up for days. . . .' They were plenty concerned about Boomer, but hadn't even the courtesy to say a word about Hobie's condition. Well, they were men of business. Boomer's skills held importance to them; a wandering cowboy's health, none.

A soft voice spoke to Hobie from the porch. He looked up, recognizing Allen Pierce, the company assayer. The white-haired old man stood holding an envelope in his gnarled hands. He was studying Hobie through the wire-rimmed spectacles he wore.

'She left you a letter, Hobie Lee,' Pierce said.

'Trish? How could she know I'd be coming back?'

'I don't know that she did, but she left this for you,' Pierce said, handing it over. He added, 'Don't be too furious with Tyrone Schaeffer and Suggs. They think you talked Miss Patricia into running away on them. And times are hard enough on the Wonder just now.'

Hobie had no feelings for the Wonder, its problems, or anyone working there just now. He managed to crawl into the saddle of his paint pony with a deal of effort. The narrow man who had taken Hobie's guns was still idling in the yard. Hobie yelled at him.

'You! I'm leaving now. I'll have my guns back.'

'Yes, sir,' the man said and he limped away toward the outbuilding.

Hobie was still having trouble breathing when he rode away toward the crossroads. He drew up the horse near the Wonder Mine sign and allowed the horse to nibble at the new grass while he remained in the saddle, opening the letter Trish had left for him with swollen, trembling fingers.

Dear Mr Hobie Lee

It looks as if the Wonder Mine is playing out faster than anyone had anticipated. The ore we're taking out is all pretty low-grade. Schaeffer and Suggs are hoping to find a new vein, but for now all we're doing is breaking rocks. They're trying to cut unnecessary expenses, and I figured out on my own that I was one of them. I wasn't contributing much, and I'm smart enough to know that.

So it's back to Laramie I will go. I told you before that I was thinking of purchasing a shop of some kind, but I also told you that I am sort of an outdoors girl. I came up with this brilliant idea: there is a lot of unused grassland around Laramie and I have enough money to buy a few sections and stock them with shorthorn cattle.

The trouble is, Hobie Lee, I really don't know much about running a ranch. I need to find someone to manage the place for me once it is started, and so I thought I'd ask you if you knew anyone who would be interested in starting up a new ranch with me.

The mail's very slow, but if you have any idea about someone I can find to help me, please do post me a letter, or just have the man report to. . . .

Yours, very truly
Patricia Fisher.

Hobie read the letter twice and then tucked it

away in his vest pocket. He had a long way to travel, but with luck he could make it to Lassen tonight. Maybe Martha Gower would lend him a bed for another night before he continued on to Wyoming.

For he was going to Laramie no matter the trail conditions. The sun was high, the sky blue, decorated with only a few white puffball clouds. There was no wind blowing. There was a still calmness in the air.

The White Wind had blown itself out.